SUICIDE PLACE

a love story

Mrs. ALEX. McVEIGH MILLER

ITNA PRESS
Los Angeles, CA
www.itnapress.com

First serialized in the *Fireside Companion* story paper in 1895 under the title "Fly-Away Floy, the Saucy Little Darling; or, the Mystery of Suicide Place."

First published as a novel under the title *The Mystery of Suicide Place* in Cleveland, OH by the Arthur Westbrook Company in 1915.

Suicide Place: A Love Story (this edited version) Itna Press Copyright © 2025

The ITNA *ICONS* Collection

Cover design by Chris Stoddard Copyright © 2025

Suicide Place: A Love Story by Mrs. Alex. McVeigh Miller
ISBN 979-8-9989551-0-5

TRIGGER WARNING

This book contains scenes and themes related to suicide. If you are struggling with suicidal thoughts or know someone who is, please seek help. You can reach the National Suicide Prevention Lifeline at 988 or visit their website, Suicide Prevention Lifeline, for more information.

WHEN THE BEAUTIFUL Maybelle Maury, of Mount Vernon, New York, was returning in October 1894, from her tour of Europe with her chaperon, Mrs. Vere de Vere, a New York society leader, she was introduced by the latter to our hero, handsome young George Beresford, the only son of a New York millionaire.

Life on shipboard offers many temptations to flirtation, and the fascinating youth did not show himself indifferent to the challenge that Maybelle's dark, languishing eyes immediately flashed into his face. He attached himself to her party, and made lazy, languid love to the beauty all the way over.

The chaperon was delighted, and plumed herself not a little on the probable grand match she had brought about for her favorite Maybelle. She knew that the girl's mother, her own distant relative, would be overjoyed at this lucky turn of Fortune's wheel. Maybelle was nineteen, and it was time she was making her matrimonial market, because she had two younger sisters at school who must come out in a year or two more, and it would be so expensive having three girls in society at once, for the father, though a prosperous New York merchant, could not be rated among the millionaires.

Our space, however, will not permit us to follow the progress of Maybelle's flirtation through those bright October days upon the sea.

But when the twain parted in New York, George Beresford was invited to visit the beauty at her home in Mount Vernon, close to the great metropolis, and carelessly promised to go "someday."

It was a shame that the handsome rogue forgot all about it afterward, so that they did not meet again until the winter, when Maybelle was spending a month in the height of the season with her New York friend, Mrs. Vere de Vere.

Her dark eyes flashed with pleasure as they clasped hands again after those months of separation, and she cried reproachfully:

"You forgot your promise!"

The laughing brown eyes grew soft with repentance as he returned, coaxingly:

"Indeed, I meant to come to Mount Vernon, but—I went South the first of November with my folks, and didn't return until—well, *recently*. So now—will you forgive me?"

Would she not forgive the deceitful wretch anything, charming Maybelle, who secretly adored him? She knew that he had only remained South five weeks, but she flashed him a melting glance, and murmured, sweetly:

"I'll forgive you, sir, on only one condition—that you come in the early spring."

"Only too glad to promise—so good of you to permit me," cooed the *jeunesse dorée,* and so the flirtation was resumed, although not very spiritedly on his part. He was five-and-twenty, and several years in the social swim had made him shy of pretty anglers for rich catches.

They met at balls, operas, and receptions—they drove together a few times, he made several short calls, and sent her flowers and books, but his frank nonchalance through it all was not encouraging. It was froth on a light wave, and even the keen attention of Mrs. Vere de Vere could detect no latent earnestness.

"He does not seem to mean anything in particular," she confided candidly to the girl on the last day of her stay, and Maybelle laughed and answered that she did not care—she had only been flirting with him.

But that night her pillow was wet with tears because of his careless farewell when he heard she was going.

But she could not banish his image from her warm heart. Her love, as well as her pride, was enlisted, and a little spark of hope kept alive in her heart the longing that he would keep his promise to come in the spring.

But it is more than probable that he would have audaciously forgotten again, only her brother Otho sought his acquaintance and attached himself to him, with the result that he "bagged the game"—that is, he brought George Beresford to Mount Vernon in May, when the handsome home on Prospect Avenue, Chester Hill, was looking its best among its trees and flowers.

Oh, how shyly happy Maybelle was at his coming! The love in her heart made her dusky beauty more dazzling than ever before. Joy lent a deeper, fuller cadence to her musical voice. Hope shone again like a brilliant star in her languishing dark eyes, with their heavy, black-fringed lashes.

George Beresford suddenly found her winning on him in a subtle fashion and told himself that really she was growing more charming with each day and hour. This tenderness and admiration might have ripened into passion for Maybelle, if only—

Ah! those words, *if only*—so short, so simple, yet so fraught with meaning!

Maybelle might have won Beresford's heart and become his bride, *if only* he had not seen, as he lounged at the gate with Otho Maury, one May morning, that vision of a blue-eyed, golden-haired, cherry-lipped, dimpled-faced girl in dark blue flashing past the gate on a shining wheel, leaving in his heart a memory of the sweetest, sauciest, most adorable young face in the world.

"Who is she?" he asked, hoarsely, of Otho, who replied, carelessly:

"Florence Fane, the carpenter's daughter, nicknamed Flyaway Floy, by reason of her hoidenish ways and never did a girl deserve the title more."

It was that lovely face, dear reader, that brought the elements of tragedy into my story.

OTHO MAURY'S TONE was light and contemptuous, but at heart he was furious. He had a *penchant* for Florence Fane himself, and dreaded a rival in this man whose face had paled at the sight of her, and whose voice had trembled as he asked her name—ay, whose very heart shone in his splendid eyes as he leaned over the gate watching the flying wheel and its graceful rider like one in a dream—a dream of love, for his pulse beat fast, his heart leaped wildly, his very soul was stirred within him in strange, delirious ecstasy.

Maybelle came down the graveled walk to them, beautiful in a dainty white gown with purple lilacs at her slender waist.

But George Beresford did not turn to meet her gaze, and Otho said, sneeringly:

"Beresford has been struck dumb by the sight of a beauty on a bicycle."

"A beauty?" frowningly.

"Yes. Little Fly-away Floy."

"Nonsense, *she* is no beauty, only a mischievous little hoiden! Don't let her turn your head, George. She isn't in *our* set at all. Her father is a mechanic, and her mother a seamstress."

"Ah!" he exclaimed, carelessly, turning around and flashing her a bright, quizzical glance, in which he seemed to dismiss the thought of Florence Fane.

He was very proud, and did not wish her to know that he had been fascinated by one so far below him in social position.

But Maybelle had equivocated, and she hoped ardently that he would not find it out.

A flavor of romance and mystery hung around Florence Fane's origin.

John Banks, the kind-hearted carpenter, had taken the sobbing child nine years ago from the side of her dead mother and carried her home to his childless wife, who, because Floy seemed to have no kith or kin, had taken her into her heart and called her daughter, and both lavished a world of tenderness on the seven-year-old child. But save in nobility of nature and a tender heart, she was no more like the homely pair than a restless hummingbird is like a toiling honeybee. She was rarely, exquisitely beautiful, lovable after an imperious fashion, but willful and untamable in disposition, the result of spoiling by a too fond and overindulgent mother, who at the last had deserted her by fleeing from life's pains and penalties by the forbidden path of suicide.

Floy was heiress by her birth to a small estate and to a terrible taint of blood—the mania for suicide.

She was a descendant of the Nellest family, that for forty years had numbered in each decade a suicide among its members.

The scene of these tragedies was at an old farmhouse on a lonely road two miles from Mount Vernon.

The house, a substantial and somewhat pretentious structure of rough dark stone, overgrown picturesquely in many places with creeping ivy, stood back from the road in a magnificent grove of old oak-trees, and twenty-five acres of rich farming land stretched away in the rear.

But so grewsome was the reputation of the place, that for nine years it had had no tenants, and its name had changed, by tacit consent of the neighborhood, from Nellest Farm to Suicide Place.

The Nellest family had owned and tilled this farm almost a hundred years, but in the middle of the century the head of the family had committed suicide by cutting his throat, and just ten years later, his only son was found hanging from a tree near the spot where his father died.

The widow of the son, with her only daughter, continued to reside at the farm, employing a competent man to manage it. But when another decade rolled around, the neighborhood was horrified to learn that the manager had shot himself in the head, adding the third to the list of deaths by suicidal mania.

Horrified and unnerved by all these tragedies, Widow Nellest fled from the place with her beautiful young daughter, leaving the property in the hands of a lawyer for rent or sale.

But neither buyer nor tenant could be found, and successive crops of weeds ripened and died on the untilled acres. The poorest beggar would have refused to live there rent-free.

At almost the end of the next decade the daughter of Widow Nellest returned to the place in widow's weeds, and with a child seven years old. Her mother had died of a broken heart, she said, and she herself had been married and widowed.

In spite of the horror of the neighborhood, she took up her abode at Suicide Place, declaring herself poor and unable to make a home elsewhere. Here she lived alone with her child, as neither manservant nor maidservant would have gone inside the gates for love or money.

And here, after a few months' solitude, Mrs. Fane, overcome by the terrible, mysterious spirit of the old place, succumbed to the mania of her family and poisoned herself.

John Banks, who had been employed by the woman to mend her gates, heard the frightened shrieks of little Floy one morning when he came to his work, and most reluctantly entered the house.

He found Mrs. Fane dead, with a bottle of poison clutched in her stiffened hand. She had been dead for hours.

The carpenter took the orphan child to his own home, and into his big, generous heart. Then he reported the case, after which there was a coroner's inquest and a verdict of suicide by poison.

Enough money was found in the house to bury her decently, and then the old place was left to its grim solitude again.

This was Florence Fane's inheritance—the old farm that none would rent or buy, and the terrible taint of blood that made her an object of a romantic interest and pity to the many who knew what must be her probable fate.

But, strange to say, the child herself knew and laughed at these whisperings. She had no superstition in her make-up, and, although forbidden by her adopted parents to enter even the gates, she was in the habit of going secretly to the old house and rambling through it at will. She even declared that she would go and live there, if anyone would bear her company, but no one accepted her defiant challenge to fate.

Meanwhile, the time was approaching when the grim, unappeasable Moloch of the place would demand, in all probability, its fifth victim. It was shunned like the plague, for all remembered that not only the family, but one of no kith or kin, had met self-sought death there. None but Floy ventured near the place—

willful Floy, who laughed to scorn their predictions that she would be the next sacrifice. When they tried to reason with her, she would not listen to their warnings, darting away like a gay, elusive little hummingbird.

When George Beresford turned away from the gate where he had watched Fly-away Floy out of sight, he knew that his heart had gone with her forever, and that he never had, and never could love Maybelle Maury as she wished to have him do—for he had long since fathomed the tender secret of her heart. The knowledge made him feel very pitiful toward the poor girl, and rendered him so abstracted that she guessed the change in him directly, and became furiously jealous of her unconscious rival, merry little Floy.

He tried to smile and chat as usual with Maybelle and Otho, but his thoughts wandered from them in spite of himself.

Oh, how strange it was—how strange! Only a careless glance from a pair of blue eyes, as the girl had smiled and nodded at Otho Maury, and all the world had changed for George Beresford. He wondered vaguely if *his glance* had made any impression on the girl's heart.

3

THE FIRST MOMENT that Maybelle was alone with Otho she clung to his arm, whispering, sorrowfully:

"Otho, I am wretched! Did you mean what you said this morning—that George admired that girl?"

"Yes, I meant it, every word, Maybelle, for it is true, curse the luck! and unless we carry things with a high hand, he is lost to you forever. In fact, I never saw a fellow so hard hit in all my life. He actually turned white to the lips with emotion, and his voice was hoarse and strange as he demanded her name, and, of course, you noticed how *distrait* and half-hearted he has been all day?"

"Yes, I saw it too plainly, but, oh, I cannot give him up! Oh, surely, he would not stoop to *her*—so far beneath him socially! Besides, she isn't so pretty, either—only with a babyish kind of beauty."

"Not so pretty, Maybelle! Why, now you make a fatal mistake, underrating the girl's charms. Half the fellows are raving over her style, and she could have a dozen proposals tomorrow, only she laughs them to scorn, the saucy little darling!"

"You are very enthusiastic, Otho!" she cried, suspiciously. "Perhaps you are in love with her yourself. I wish you would marry her tomorrow, and make it impossible for her to become my rival."

He flushed, then laughed, answering, coolly:

"Thank you, but the plan isn't feasible. I shouldn't mind making love to the pretty little thing, for she's sweet enough to turn any man's head, but I intend, like yourself, to marry money when I sacrifice myself on Hymen's altar."

"Oh, brother, I am wretched, wretched! It isn't alone for the money I want him. I have had other offers—rich ones, too, but I love *him*, love him, love him! I must win him or die! All in a minute I feel desperately wicked, and willing to do anything to win him for my own. I hate that girl already, and wish her dead! Why does she not go and kill herself like her mother?"

"Probably she will in the end, but she isn't unhappy enough yet."

"Then let us do something to drive her mad with despair at once!" cried Maybelle, feverishly, recklessly, her dark eyes flashing with a tigerish light not good to see.

Otho's eyes flashed back the same spirit, for his heart was burning with a cruel passion for bonny Floy. Stooping close to her ear, he whispered, hoarsely:

"Suppose I could drive her mad with love for me?"

"Try it, Otho, try it! Begin at once, please!" she responded, eagerly, hopefully.

"I will, for I fancy she admires me immensely already by her blushes when I speak to her, and I'll follow up the good impression at once, storm the castle of her fancy, as it were, with ardent lovemaking, persuade her to elope with me, perhaps—oh, a mock marriage, of course! She is poor, and so she could not be taken *au sérieux.*"

She listened without a protest to his diabolical scheme for wrecking the life of a pure and lovely girl. Oh, a jealous woman can be so hard and pitiless!

He continued:

"Of course you know she will be at the picnic we attend to-morrow?"

"No! Who dared invite the creature?" imperiously.

"Pshaw! Maybelle, that scorn was well acted before Beresford today, but in private we know that the girl really has some rights and a sort of footing in our set, so that we're apt to meet her at less exclusive functions, such as this picnic will be. We cannot keep from meeting her tomorrow, but we can forestall Beresford's suit by plotting beforehand."

"Tell me how, Otho, and be sure I will act my part."

"I am sure you will, but I must first think it over, and in the morning I will confide my plans to you before we start for the picnic. And I'll call at the carpenter's cottage this evening. She is always on the porch with her guitar. I'll get in her good graces so that I can monopolize her company tomorrow, and make him think he has no show with her at all. I'll throw in some little fibs, too, that he's engaged to you, etc., so that she will shun him."

"Yes, Otho, I see. That is a splendid idea, and easy to carry out. Oh, how I thank you for your clever help all through!" she cried, in a transport of joy and gratitude.

Otho accepted the praise complacently, but he knew he was working more for himself than for her.

It would be a most delightful part to play, the making love to Floy, and as for the rest, he was heart and soul in the scheme to win a millionaire for his brother-in-law. He was selfish and extravagant, and always in hot water with his father about money, so when Maybelle secured her prize he would make her pay a heavy price for his help.

4

THE NEXT MORNING dawned gloriously, and in due time the carriages reached the picnic-grounds—just a mile past Suicide Place—a picturesque grove on the banks of a river. There was a pavilion and music for dancing, with every device for pleasure.

And Floy was there with the rest, charming in a white duck suit and big hat, self-possessed as a young princess, and not one whit abashed when Otho led her to his party, and said, graciously:

"You know my sister Maybelle, don't you? She has been away a great deal lately, but she remembers little Fly-away Floy, and this is my friend, Mr. George Beresford."

They all bowed graciously, and then the quartet sat down together on the riverbank, for all this condescension was the plot that wicked Otho had unfolded to his sister that morning. Other couples joined them, while some danced in the pavilion, and still others swung in the hammocks under the shady trees.

They talked lightly and desultory on frothy subjects, as people at picnics usually do, and barely anyone but Beresford remembered afterward that it was Otho Maury who started the subject of bravery and courage, and contrasted the difference in man and woman on these qualities of mind and strength. He exclaimed, finally:

"I adore courage and bravery in man or woman. Indeed, I would not marry a girl who was a coward—who ran shrieking from a mouse, or trembled at the thought of a burglar—but I could worship a fearless girl, such a one, for instance, as would dare to spend a night alone in a haunted house."

The pretty girls who heard him all shrieked and shuddered with dismay—all except Floy, who shrugged her pretty shoulders, and said, vivaciously:

"Pshaw! that is not any great thing to do. I shouldn't be afraid to stay in a haunted house all night."

"Aren't you afraid of ghosts, like most young girls?" asked Otho, incredulously.

"No, I'm not afraid, for I don't believe in spirits."

Maybelle laughed tauntingly.

"You are joking, Floy. You wouldn't dare stay alone all night in Suicide House—now, would you?"

The girls all applauded Maybelle, sneering at Floy's pretense of bravery, until the impulsive girl saw that they were overtly challenging her to a proof of her courage.

Flushing with anger, her blue eyes blazing with defiance, she cried, stormily:

"I am not a coward, Maybelle Maury, and I am not afraid of anything, ghost or human, and I will prove it to you all by staying alone at Suicide House tonight!"

"No, no, you must not!" cried a few voices, frightened at the thought of what she had been goaded to do.

But Floy's high spirit was up in arms, and she would not be dissuaded from her purpose.

"I shall surely do it, and no one shall prevent me!" she cried, adding: "When we go home tonight, you may leave me at Suicide Place, and I will lock myself in, for I have the keys with me now, and you can go by and tell auntie I stayed all night with one of the girls. In the morning you may send a committee to escort me home in triumph. Why do you all look so pale and frightened? There is no danger, I tell you. I've been over the house a hundred times alone, and the only ghosts are rats. It will be rare fun staying there all night!"

No one could dissuade her, so they gave up trying. Everybody was sorry for it, but Otho and his sister, who exchanged furtive looks of satisfaction.

George Beresford had not spoken a word during the whole conversation, though his eager, admiring eyes had scarcely left Floy's lovely flower-like face. He was silent, abstracted, bitterly piqued at Floy's pronounced indifference to himself.

She had not seemed to see him since the first glance in which she had acknowledged their introduction by Otho Maury, and of course he could not know that it was because Otho had said to her at the cottage gate last night:

"My sister Maybelle will be at the picnic tomorrow with her handsome betrothed—the rich New Yorker she is to marry this fall. She is as jealous of him as a little Turk, and it makes her angry for any other girl to even look at him."

He had counted rightly on Floy's high sense of honor.

She was a mischievous little madcap, but she respected Maybelle's rights, and feigned indifference to Beresford, although she could not avoid noticing the ardent glance he threw in her direction, and she thought, indignantly:

"No wonder Maybelle is jealous, for I can see already that he's a wretched flirt. I won't even look at him, though he is awfully, awfully handsome!"

So with a sigh, whose subtle meaning she could not understand, she turned her back on the wretched Beresford, and entered readily into an animated conversation with Otho, maddening her silent admirer with such keen jealousy that he could bear it no longer.

"Let us go and dance," he said to Maybelle, hoarsely.

"Oh, I'm too lazy to move. Go and find another partner," she laughed.

"But I'm not acquainted with any of the girls here."

"Otho, go along and introduce him to some girls, and I'll stay with Floy and tell her about my lovely trip to Europe last year."

Beresford, disappointed in a faint hope that she might have proffered Floy to him as a partner, went away with Otho, and Maybelle made herself agreeable to her companion.

At last she observed, patronizingly:

"You've never been *anywhere*, have you, Floy?"

"Not since mamma brought me a little girl back to the farm," Floy answered, flushing sensitively, for she felt the sting in Maybelle's patronizing tone.

But the latter continued, gently and purringly:

"It's too bad your having to stay with those poor, hard-working people, isn't it? Shouldn't you like to support yourself, Floy?"

"I should not know how to earn a penny," murmured Floy, who was like the naughty Brier-Rose of the poem:

Whene'er a thrifty matron this idle maid espied,
She shook her head in warning and scarce her wrath could hide;
For girls were made for housewives, for spinning-wheel and loom,
And not to drink the sunshine and the flowers' sweet perfume.
But out she skipped the meadows o'er and gazed into the sky,

Her heart o'erbrimmed with gladness, she scarce herself knew why;
And to a merry tune she hummed: 'Oh, Heaven only knows
Whatever will become of the naughty Brier-Rose?'

"Suppose I tell you what papa was saying about you last night?" continued Maybelle.

"Yes," Floy answered, helplessly.

"He was saying that he needed two new salesgirls in his big dry-goods store in New York, and he wondered if any girls in Mount Vernon would like to go. He said he had thought of you, and that maybe old John Banks would be glad to have you find a situation and help earn your own living."

Floy reddened, paled, then gasped:

"I don't believe Uncle John would like it at all. He loves me— he and auntie—and he doesn't mind taking care of me."

"But you'll tell him of this offer, won't you, dear, and you'll think of it yourself? Papa says he'll keep the place open a week for you," said Maybelle, who had suggested the plan to Otho herself.

"I'll tell Uncle John," promised Floy, but she seemed tongue-tied after that, and went moodily away from Maybelle's vicinity to join some other girls, keeping so resolutely away that they did not meet again until that afternoon, when most of the dancers were resting after dinner on the banks of the beautiful river.

At heart Floy was cruelly wounded by Maybelle's patronizing, but she was too proud to show her pain. Once George Beresford ventured to seek her for a partner in the dance, but she refused so curtly that he turned away indignantly, wondering why she was so cold to him while so kind to others.

"She has plenty of smiles for that shallow Otho. I'd like to wring his little black neck!" he thought, angrily.

Otho was a cur, indeed, but he was slight and dark and elegant—one of those types that very young girls rave over. Beresford saw that he stood high in Floy's good graces, and began to hate him accordingly.

When the couples paired off on the riverbank beneath the shady trees, there was Maybelle and Beresford, and next to them Floy and Otho.

Floy was bright and restless, feeling Beresford's gaze ever seeking hers, and wondering why it thrilled her so when she knew it was not right for him to look at any other than Maybelle, his beautiful, dark-eyed betrothed.

She turned her back on him rather rudely, and exclaimed to Otho:

"People are very foolish and superstitious. They are always going on about Suicide Place, and saying that it must claim another victim soon, and they are even hinting that I will be the doomed one."

"That is nonsense. I am sure you are too strong-minded to yield to such a temptation," Otho replied, reassuringly.

George could not help listening to the sound of the musical voice and watching the beautiful profile when it turned toward him in her animated talk.

Heavens, how lovely she was! What eyes, what lips, what dimples, what a mesh of curly, golden hair in which to entangle a man's throbbing heart! And yet it was not simply her beauty that enthralled him, and he knew it. She had that psychical charm we call personal magnetism, that is like the perfume to the flower and seems to endow it with a soul.

He heard her continue, almost defiantly, as if annoyed:

"I wish they would not talk about it, for it makes me angry. Why should I kill myself? I'm young and gay, and, in a way, happy! And yet," musingly, "I suppose, after all, that the terrible taint of that mania is in my blood. I am not superstitious, but perhaps it may conquer me after all, who knows? Do you suppose I shall ever kill myself?"

"I hope not. You would break a dozen hearts if you did, mine among the rest," Otho replied, banteringly, with a killing glance.

She continued, meditatively:

"They will go on expecting me to commit suicide, of course, and always selecting the old farm as the scene of the fifth tragedy. Why should I not choose some other scene for the final act? This river, say," pointing to it as it rippled below the bank, dark and deep and dangerous in its beauty.

Laughing, she rose to her feet, and he said:

"It seems that fate always demands the sacrifice within the gates of the grim old place."

"Do you think so? Well, I shall defy the fate to which I was born, and break the charm of Suicide Place. If, following the taint in my blood, I must indeed kill myself, I shall disappoint everybody in the location. It shall not be at the old farm, but—*here!*"

Then all at once the startling tragedy happened.

Floy stepped to the edge of the bank with a strange, mocking laugh on her red lips, and, as if the terrible mania had seized on her suddenly, red-handed and implacable as fate itself, she threw up her arms above her beautiful head, and leaped into the river that divided hungrily to receive the girlish form, then closed again greedily over its prey.

5

PRETTY FLOY'S STARTLING, unexpected, and terrible action produced the effect of a thunderclap on the gay and thoughtless crowd of young people who witnessed it.

A moment of blank, awed silence ensued, then everyone seemed to join in a cry of alarm and dismay as they pressed forward to the banks and watched the eddying circles of water over the deep and dangerous spot where that lovely form had disappeared from view.

They watched eagerly for the golden head to reappear.

Meanwhile, Otho Maury sat motionless gazing at the water, his face marble-white, but in his eyes, beneath their lowered lids, a strange and devilish gleam of joy, as he thought to himself:

"How deuced clever in the little girl to hasten the *dénouement* of her life like this! It saves Maybelle and me a world of trouble."

As for Maybelle, when Floy sprung into the water, she uttered one loud, hysterical shriek, and clutched her companion with both hands, hiding her dark eyes against his shoulder as though she could not bear the sight of the river.

But in an instant Beresford recovered from his trance of horror, and struggled to release himself and rise.

But Maybelle clung to him so wildly that he could not loosen her grasp without hurting the clinging white hands.

"Do not leave me—do not leave me, George! I am so frightened!" she wailed, beseechingly.

"Otho! Otho!" called Beresford, sternly, and as Maury looked around with a dazed expression, he added: "Come to your sister—I must save that girl!"

Otho did not stir from his position, pretending not to understand, and Maybelle tightened her frantic clutch until he saw that he must use gentle force to release himself.

"I beg your pardon, but in common humanity I must go," he said, resolutely, and wrenched himself free, rushing forward, throwing off his coat and hat as he went. Then, amid ringing cheers, the big, handsome fellow plunged into the river.

Out of that crowd of perhaps fifty young men he was the only one that had volunteered to save the drowning girl, although half a score of them had pretended to adore her.

As Beresford sprung into the water, Floy's little head suddenly appeared above it some distance away from where she had sunk. He struck out in that direction, shouting to her to be brave, that he would save her life.

But at the sound of his voice, the girl's head suddenly sunk beneath the water again, as though she were determined to accomplish her purpose of suicide.

Our hero, swimming with strong and gallant strokes toward the spot, made a bold dive down to the depths, but rose again without Floy.

Directly her head bobbed up again some distance off, but swimming quickly toward her, Beresford grasped her where she lay easily floating on the water, not having realized in his excitement that she had been swimming furtively under the water, leading him a race for the fun of the thing, for she was not in the least danger.

Grasping her tightly, he said in hoarse tones, broken with joyful emotion:

"Thank Heaven, I reached you before you sunk again! It was a terrible thing you attempted, but I shall save you in spite of yourself."

Floy laughed softly, and answered in a meek little voice:

"Oh, I'm sorry now that I did it. I don't believe I want to die after all!"

"That is right," he cried, heartily. "Now, be calm, and I will take you safely to the shore. Put your hands on my shoulder easily, like this," placing them. "Be cool, and don't get frightened and clutch at me—above all, don't clasp my neck, for the current is very deep and strong, and you must not impede my motions. Do you understand?"

"Oh, yes, and I'll do as you say. I—I should have liked to hold you around the neck, but if you object to it so seriously, I won't."

Was there a tone of exquisite raillery in the girl's voice? He looked suspiciously into her face, and saw veiled mischief in the clear blue eyes. She was not frightened—not in the least.

"Thank you," he returned, coolly, but with a fast-beating heart. "I am sure the experience would be delightful, and if you like to try it after we are safe on land, I shall be most happy."

"I hate you!" pouted Floy, and letting her hands slip, sunk again below the surface.

Terribly alarmed, he dived and brought her safely to the surface once more, saying, sternly:

"Do not be so careless again, or you may lose your life."

To his amazement, she laughed mockingly.

"Swim on and I'll keep by your side. Don't be alarmed over me, for I've been doing all this for a purpose. I can swim like a fish."

And, to his wonder and chagrin, for he felt himself grow hot even in the cold water with the thought that he had suddenly been turned from a conquering hero into an object of ridicule, Fly-away Floy, the merry little madcap, swam along by his side as easily and gracefully as a beautiful mermaid, until they reached the bank, when he gave her his hand to assist her, and they came again upon *terra firma*, greeted by admiring cheers from the onlookers.

While they were in the water, Otho had hurried to Maybelle, and whispered, hoarsely:

"Why didn't you hold him tighter, you little fool? If you could have kept him from going to her assistance a short time, she would have been drowned and out of your way."

"I knew it, and I tried to keep him back, but he shook me off in a rage, and I—I'm sure he even swore at me under his breath," whimpered Maybelle, despairingly.

"Very likely," grumbled Otho, and then he turned from her to watch Beresford's progress, and saw to his amazement the man and girl clambering up the bank.

In the silence that followed the rousing cheer of joy at their return, Floy turned to her dripping cavalier, saying demurely:

"I thank you from my heart, George, for your noble attempt to save my life. I was not in any danger, it is true, for I can swim like a duck, but of course you did not know that, and you are just as truly a real hero as if your brave attempts had indeed saved me from a watery grave."

There was a swelling murmur of surprise from all around her, and one little girl, bolder than the rest, came up and said:

"Why, Floy, didn't you intend to drown yourself after all?"

Floy tossed back her wet curly mass of short ringlets, and returned merrily:

"Of course not, little goosy. Why should I be so silly as to kill myself, I that am so young and happy? I only jumped in to frighten you all—yes, and to test the courage of a gentleman who told us only this morning how much he adored physical courage."

Her accusing blue eyes turned on Otho Maury, and she said, with light, laughing scorn:

"I thought as you pretended to be so very, very fond of me, that you would risk your life to save mine, but you proved yourself a coward after all!"

He was livid with secret, sullen rage, but putting a bold face on the matter, he answered, carelessly:

"Oh, I knew it was only a trick, and that you could swim as well as anybody, so I didn't choose to humor your fancy to have me jump in the water and ruin my new fifty-dollar suit, like my friend Beresford here, who, it's plain to be seen, is as mad as a March hare at the way he was fooled. Come, *mon ami*, shall I drive you into town for some dry clothes?"

"If you please," returned Beresford, who was indeed bitterly chagrined at being made the butt of such a joke, and angrily conscious of cutting such a poor figure among them all in his drenched clothing. He picked up his hat and coat and went away with Otho, who returned alone within the hour, saying that Beresford was in the sulks and wouldn't come back.

"And as for you, little mischief," he said, banteringly, to Floy, who had been over to a house close by and borrowed a pretty suit, in which she reappeared as fresh as a rose—"as for you, the lordly Beresford will never forgive you for making him appear ridiculous by jumping into the river to rescue a girl who could swim as well as he could. He said he should have liked to shake you for a naughty, saucy little vixen."

"Who cares?" returned Floy, gayly, not the least abashed by George's resentment.

When the picnic was over, Maybelle slyly reminded her of her promise about Suicide Place.

"Oh, yes, I'm going to spend the night there, certainly," she replied, and left the carriage at the gates of the grim old house, in spite of the remonstrances of many of the party, who were really uneasy at the thought of such a daring adventure.

Floy would not listen to any of them. She answered them with careless, merry banter, and as the carriages rolled away, they saw her standing inside the gates, waving her little hand in farewell, her slender, white-robed figure clearly defined in the gloom of the falling twilight.

6

MERRY LITTLE FLOY went dancing like a sunbeam through the dark oak grove, and sat down to rest on the porch before she entered the house for her night's vigil.

She rested there while the full moon rose over the tree-tops, silvering the scene with an unearthly light, and throwing fantastic leaf-shadows on the short green grass. It was like an enchanted palace, so calm, so quiet, undisturbed by any sound save the plaintive call of a whip-poor-will away off in the dim, silent woods.

She mused a little soberly on the events of the day.

"That big coward, Otho Maury, I was beginning to fancy myself in love with him, but—I despise him now!" curving a red, disdainful lip. "And how I fooled them all! They really thought I was attempting suicide! Ha, ha! But how splendid Maybelle's *fiancé* was, how brave, how cool, and if only—he wasn't engaged, I believe I should have lost my heart to him—so there!"

Perhaps she *had* lost her heart to him anyway, in spite of Maybelle, for she could not get the thought of the big, handsome, brown-eyed fellow out of her little curly head, and she recalled with a sudden warm wave of color rushing to her face the audacious frankness of the words he had said to her in the water, answering her saucy jest:

"I'm sure the experience would be delightful, and if you like to try it when we are safe on land, I shall be most happy."

Floy had thrilled with sweet ecstasy at his daring words, and now she said, audaciously:

"Yes, I—I *should* like to try it! I should throw my arms around his big neck and hug him tight, and kiss his sweet, brave lips, the beautiful hero, only—" and the words trailed off into a deep sigh at the sudden thought of Maybelle, who stood between them.

And like a dash of cold water came the memory of Otho's words.

Beresford was angry with her for the joke she had played, and would like to shake her for a naughty, saucy little vixen.

"Let him try it—that's all!" she exclaimed, shaking her bright head defiantly, then leaning it half despondently on her arm.

Wearied by the pleasures of the long, bright day, she sunk into slumber.

Sweet dreams came to her there in the fragrant gloom of the warm spring night.

To her fancy she was walking with George Beresford in a beautiful rose garden.

Overhead there leaned a sky all darkly, beautifully blue, while little fleecy clouds tempered the golden brightness of noon.

From afar there came to her the soft murmur of the sea blended with low, soft music divinely sweet and tender—the music of love.

All around her were the rarest roses filling the summer air with fragrance—roses intwining shady bowers of latticework, roses wreathing triumphal arches, roses bordering long winding walks, delicious thickets of roses so dense that the sun's rays had not yet dried the dew from their velvet petals.

On her head was a wreath of pink roses, at the waist of her beautiful fleecy white gown, were white and pink ones blended in exquisite contrast.

By her side, with his arm about her slender, supple waist, walked handsome George Beresford.

They were lovers.

And in this beautiful rose garden they seemed to be as much alone as Adam and Eve were in Eden.

No faintest sound of the great surging, wicked world intruded on the delicious solitude—nothing came to their hearing save the low murmur of the distant sea, that soft music breathing the soul of love, and the song of birds mating and nesting in the rose-trees that shook down their bloomy petals in rosy clouds over every path.

They did not miss nor want the world in this Eden. They were all in all to each other, this beautiful pair of lovers.

They roamed here and there with their arms about each other, speaking but little, only now and then Beresford would pause to draw her into his arms and caress her, murmuring between ardent kisses: "My only love, my bride!"

Beautiful, dark-eyed, jealous Maybelle Maury was forgotten just as entirely as though she had never existed. They were blissfully happy in this dream that Floy was dreaming there that May night in the grim shadow of Suicide Place.

But suddenly a dark, portentous cloud overspread the sky, and a low rumble of thunder shook the earth.

The soft voice of the sea changed to a hollow roar, as though a storm were lashing its waves into fury, and the tender music wailed itself into silence like the cry of a broken heart. The winds rose and lashed the rose-trees in a furious gale, till the air was full of their flying petals and spicy perfumes. The songbirds fled affrighted, and their little nests were dashed upon the ground.

"Oh, I am so frightened! Save me!" sobbed pretty Floy, clinging to her fond lover, who clasped and kissed her again, whispering that there was no danger for her while he was by his little darling's side.

But at that very moment a flash of lightning irradiated the gloom, and Floy saw a woman dashing toward her in insane fury.

She had the dark, beautiful, jealous face of Maybelle Maury, and she rushed between them and thrust Floy away.

"Go, girl, go! He is mine, mine, mine!" she was crying, madly, when all at once Floy awoke, as we do in dreams at some moment of unbearable grief and woe.

Her dream had been only half a dream, after all.

The moonlight was darkened by clouds, there was low, rumbling thunder, followed by flashes of lightning, and a fitful rain was driven into the porch by the wayward wind, wetting Floy's face and hands and dress. It was this that had woven itself in with her dream and awakened her to unpleasant reality.

Dazed and wondering, she sprung to her feet, and it was several minutes before she could realize her position.

Then it came to her that Maybelle had dared her to spend a night alone at Suicide Place, and she had vowed she would do it.

She had come and fallen asleep on the porch and dreamed that exquisite dream that was so lovely until—Maybelle came.

"How strange that I should dream of Maybelle's lover—and dream that he was *mine!*" she murmured, wonderingly, as she hurried into the house out of the muttering storm.

Fortunately she had brought some matches, and she knew that there was a lamp in the parlor, so letting herself in, she hurriedly lighted the lamp, throwing its feeble glare on the dark oak furniture of the long apartment.

"Whew! what a musty old place!" she ejaculated, throwing open a window, heedless of the fine mist of rain that came blowing in, mixed with delicious fresh air and gusts of delicate perfume from great lilac-trees outside loaded with white and purple blooms.

Then she uttered a cry of dismay and looked back half fearfully over her shoulder at a piano in a dark corner.

The lid was closed, but from the keys were coming low, discordant sounds, as of music played by childish hands all ignorant of time or tune. It was terrible, that sound, and Floy, who had never known fear before, felt as if ice-cold water were trickling down her spine.

Then a quick suspicion came to her, and running straight to the instrument, she threw back the lid.

Several mice that, alarmed by her entrance, had been running up and down the keys, producing discordant notes, jumped out upon the floor and ran away into the dark corners with little frightened squeaks.

Floy laughed aloud merrily:

"Just as I suspected, after my first moment of terror at that sudden sound. But a cowardly person would have sworn it was a ghost playing the piano. I wonder if that discord was the sweet music I heard in my dream?"

She threw herself into a large easy chair cushioned in leather, and closed her eyes.

"I am not the least bit afraid—not the least," she declared aloud. "But I wish I could go to sleep again and dream the first half of that lovely dream."

But slumber refused to visit her eyes again. She felt preternaturally wide awake.

Rising, she paced up and down the room, listening to the muttering of the storm outside, and the wild rain driving against the creaking old windows.

Several old family portraits hung against the walls, and the eyes of those buried ancestors seemed to follow her up and down with grim curiosity as she moved to and fro.

Such a thing will seriously annoy one sometimes. The eyes of a portrait may take on a living look, and render one horribly nervous when alone at midnight.

Those following eyes, so persistent in their stare, annoyed Floy, and gave her the same creepy chill down her back that she had felt when the mice scurried over the piano keys.

She could not resist a sudden longing to escape from the room, and from the grim scrutiny of her pictured ancestors.

Taking the lamp in her hand, she started out to explore the house.

Hurrying along the draughty hall, and in and out of the musty old rooms familiar to her childhood, the girl tried to dispel the shadow that began to fall on her spirits like an ominous cloud.

Presently, over the roar of the storm outside, her voice rang out in a loud, wild, terrified shriek thrice repeated— then awful silence.

7

HALF AN HOUR passed by slowly.

The storm was over.

The lightning, thunder, and rain had ceased, and the moon was coming out from the black wrack of clouds where she had hidden her glory.

Her silver light shone again upon the sleeping world, and flashed into the parlor window that Floy had opened before she left the room half an hour ago.

In the sheen of the moonlight, the staring eyes of the portraits on the wall seemed to be watching eagerly for their descendant to reappear.

The hall door opened softly, and Floy staggered across the threshold, bearing the lamp unsteadily in her small hand.

What a change had come over the sparkling *riante* face!

She was pale to the lips—pale as a ghost, as the saying goes—and there was a strange expression in her blue eyes, as if they had looked upon something uncanny.

With an unsteady step, as though she trembled in every limb, the lamp flaring dismally in her grasp, she dragged herself across the room to a long swinging mirror between the windows, and held the light up over her golden head, looking at herself carefully, as she whispered:

"I wonder if my hair has turned white?"

The words, coupled with her appalling shrieks of half an hour ago, proved two facts. First, that Floy had sustained a severe shock of some kind, since only sudden fright or grief is supposed to whiten the hair in a single hour, and secondly, that she was recovering from her alarm, as manifested by her anxiety over her personal appearance.

The long mirror gave her back faithfully the beautiful form with the graceful swelling curves of dawning womanhood, and the lovely face lighted by clear blue eyes, and crowned by waves of crinkly gold above the frank white brow.

No, her hair had not turned white, despite the untold horror that had shaken her soul to the center. Not even one silver thread shone among the gold.

Floy heaved a long, bursting sigh of intense relief, set down the lamp, and dropped wearily into a chair near the window.

The moon's rays shone in her white face, so pale and horror-struck, and she saw that the storm was over and the sky clear again.

"Oh, how much longer must I stay here? —how long before the dawn?" she muttered, fearfully, gazing straight before her into the night, as if afraid to look back into the grewsome room with its dark, shadowy corners.

And this was Fly-away Floy, the fearless, with her nerves of steel, and her contemptuous disbelief in the supernatural—this pale, startled creature who had just looked into the mirror to see if the golden locks of youth had changed to the frosty ones of age.

What had changed and shaken the careless girl like this? Would she ever reveal the secret? Or would her indomitable pride seal her lips?

She leaned out of the window, reaching down and breaking off great clusters of wet, fragrant lilacs, in which she buried her stricken face, while low, bursting sobs convulsed her form—sobs of abject misery.

Hark! what was that sound? Only the low wind of the summer night soughing through the trees.

"No," she cried, dismissing the fancy and springing to her feet, "it is a step in the hall!"

She clung to the windowsill, looking over her shoulder with terrified blue eyes, her heart beating wildly against her side.

She was half tempted to spring from the window and seek refuge in flight.

But it was at least ten feet from the ground, and she did not fancy the idea of making a cripple of herself.

The door was suddenly flung open, and a laughing voice exclaimed, eagerly:

"Where are you, Floy?"

The very sound of a human voice was bliss to her after the long and fearful night.

She sprung up, sobbing with joy and relief, as Otho Maury entered the room with a lantern.

"So you have come for me! I—I didn't guess it was near daylight yet," she faltered.

"It isn't, Floy—only a little past midnight."

He came up to her with a jubilant air, and his eager, dark eyes burned on her face as he continued:

"But I couldn't rest for thinking of you, Floy, all alone in this terrible place, exposed to Heaven knows what dangers! I—I—my heart ached for your loneliness, dear little one, and so I came to share your vigil."

At the first moment her face had brightened with relief, but when he came up close she drew back shrinkingly, and at his words she took swift alarm.

"You have been frightened. I knew you would be, though you pretended to be so brave. I see the tears on your lashes. Now, aren't you glad I came?" triumphantly.

"Yes, I'm glad, for I did wrong to come. I've grown nervous waiting here alone, and you may take me home at once," she answered, gratefully, throwing on her hat and turning toward the door.

"Wait a little, Floy, for there's a storm coming up. I did not think you would want to go until daylight, when the committee called for you with a carriage."

She recoiled, looking at him with startled eyes.

"Do you mean to say that they did not come with you—that you came here alone?" she demanded.

"Why, yes, that was what I told you, Floy. I feared the storm would frighten you, so I came to remain with you till morning."

The wet lilacs at the window shook and rustled as in a rising gale, but neither heeded it in their excitement.

He pressed closer, and tried to take her hand, but she drew herself to her full height, the color rushing to her pale cheeks, her eyes like blue fire.

"Go! leave me at once!" she commanded, imperiously.

"Leave you, Floy—I cannot! Did you not confess just now that you had grown nervous waiting here alone? And there were tears on your lovely cheeks when I found you drooping here. No, darling, I shall stay and cheer your solitude."

"Is the man mad, or does he think me an ignorant child with no knowledge of the world and its ways? Listen, Otho Maury: you cannot remain here through the night with me, for what would people say tomorrow?"

She seemed to grow taller with each word so bravely spoken, as she stood before him like an imperious little queen, her finger still pointing to the door.

But the man made no motion to obey, and his manner was full of a jaunty *insouciance* that filled her with indefinable dismay.

"Nonsense!" he answered, airily, and his voice sunk to a tender cadence as he continued: "Darling little Floy, no one need know of my being here tonight. No one knew of my coming, and I can slip away just before daylight, don't you see? Then when the committee comes you will be found alone bright and happy, and they will believe your proud boast that you were not the least afraid to stay alone in Suicide Place."

"I command you to go at once!" she said, angrily.

"I refuse to obey," he returned, jauntily, and there was a streaming fire of elation in his eyes that almost drove her wild.

"Then I shall go and leave you here!" she said, scornfully, turning to the door, but he barred her way. "I can spring from the window!" she cried, moving to it, and not noticing the rustling of the lilac branches.

"And kill yourself," he sneered. "No, Floy, you will not be so rash. You will stay here with me, for I love you madly, beautiful one! and I came here to be alone with you where none could interfere, that I might clasp your lovely form to my heart and kiss your scornful lips till they yielded to my caresses, till your heart thrilled to mine with responsive love!"

"Why, I hate you! hate you! hate you! you cowardly villain, you infamous cur!" raged Floy, tempestuously, as she tried to rush past him and gain the door.

But Otho was too quick for her, agile as she was. Rushing forward, he caught her in his arms, pressing her tightly to his breast, heedless of her wild shrieks of fear and prayers for mercy.

Struggling fiercely to bend back her fair head and kiss her crimson lips, the villain did not catch the rustling sound of the branches at the window, as a man who had been hiding and listening there came at a bound over the sill and into the room.

But the next moment Otho's arms were caught in a grasp of steel, and a hoarse voice thundered:

"Release the lady, you vile hound, and take your punishment!"

It was George Beresford, raging like a lion in his fury, and as Maury's grasp on Floy relaxed, he caught up the slim, wriggling coward in his athletic grasp, shook him contemptuously, and flew over to the window.

Floy, raising up her eyes to her noble deliverer, saw him, pale with revengeful fury, as, with superb strength, he lifted Maury up to the window and hurled him through it over the tops of the lilacs far out into the grove.

8

FLOY WATCHED THE punishment of Otho Maury with that boundless admiration a woman always feels for manly strength and power.

She thought that George Beresford was the grandest, bravest, most beautiful hero in the world, and her heart swelled with gratitude to him for his manly defense of a helpless girl.

But she was frightened, too, when she saw her persecutor's body flying through the air, and she cried out, shudderingly:

"Oh, you have killed the wretch!"

But her preserver answered, coolly:

"No, indeed, more's the pity! It's only a few feet from the window to the ground. Besides, didn't you hear the thud of his body on the soft wet grass? No bones will be broken, I assure you, though it ought to be his neck. But, anyway, this will teach him a much-needed lesson!"

And he laughed softly to himself at the ease with which he had sent Maury spinning through the window.

"Oh, I thank you so much—so much! I was so frightened!" faltered Floy, clasping her white hands in the intensity of her joy, and lifting to him her beautiful, clear blue eyes.

He smiled at her kindly, thinking to himself that it was the loveliest face in the round world, and answered:

"It was rather fortunate I came when I did, for I suspected the fellow had been drinking. That was why I followed him here when I found out he was coming."

"Oh, how good you were—how good, I can never thank you enough!" cried Floy, putting out her hand to him in the exuberance of her gratitude.

Beresford clasped the little hand ardently, and longed to kiss it, but would not frighten her by such a demonstration.

"Poor little soul, she has been alarmed enough already," he thought, generously, the pale cheeks and tear-wet lashes appealing to all the manliness within him.

"And now you will take me home, will you not?" added Floy, appealingly.

"Yes, for I came here with that purpose, and my carriage is waiting at the gate. Come," he said, putting out the lamp and taking up the flaring lantern left by Otho Maury, as he moved toward the door.

Floy paused to shut down the window, and followed him, oh, so gladly, out of that horror-haunted house in the sweet moist air of the spring night, breathing a sigh of relief when she found herself going down the graveled walk, through the grove, by Beresford's side.

"Oughtn't we to see—if *he* is hurt or killed?" she murmured, timidly.

Beresford answered, carelessly:

"Oh, he is all right. I hear him coming behind us now."

And, sure enough, a voice called, humbly:

"Beresford—Floy! Will you please wait a moment?"

They paused, and saw Otho Maury limping dejectedly toward them, looking very meek in the bright moonlight that streamed through interstices of the trees.

Floy's tender little heart gave a leap of joy that he was not killed, although she knew that he well deserved it.

He dropped with difficulty on one knee before Floy, muttering:

"I crave your pardon, Floy, for my rudeness just now. I swear I meant no harm except to kiss you. But I had been drinking— and I will own it—I was mad with love for you. But I never should have frightened you so only that I had drunk too much wine and I lost my head. I'm glad Beresford threw me out of the window, for my madness deserved it, though I'm a mass of bruises, and my ankle is either sprained or broken. But that does not matter so that you forgive me. Will you?" contritely.

Floy had the tenderest heart in the world, and Otho's repentance was so frank and engaging that she hesitated.

"Do you think I ought to forgive him?" she whispered to Beresford, with a ravishing little air of reliance on his judgment!

He shrugged his shoulders, and replied, carelessly:

"Perhaps so—since he asks it."

"Very well," said Floy, and looking coldly at the offender, she said, proudly: "I forgive you, as you say you are sorry, but don't you ever dare speak to me again!"

She was turning away, with her head held high in scorn, but he caught at her sleeve.

"One moment, please. I have another favor to ask of you and—Beresford," the last word with a gulp, as if swallowing his pride with difficulty.

They both stopped to listen, and he muttered:

"Will you both keep the story of this affair a secret? It will ruin me if it becomes known. My father—he has threatened to disinherit me if I do not quit drinking. I had promised him, but I—I broke my word tonight. Then, too, the ridicule of my set—*you* know how it could sting. Beresford, for God's sake, be merciful, as you are strong and brave!"

He drooped before them—craven, abject, appealing, a cur to despise—in the moonlight.

Beresford knew that what he advanced was true. The story of tonight's offense and its punishment would make Maury the laughingstock of all who heard it—would follow him with its blight through life.

He was disposed to pity the abject suppliant, the depths of whose meanness his own noble nature could not fathom.

So he answered, after a moment's reflection:

"It shall be as the young lady says, of course, though I must say you do not merit her leniency."

"I know too well that I do not, but she is an angel, and will grant my prayer," muttered the wretched delinquent.

"No, I'm not an angel, and I hate and despise you, Otho Maury!" flashed the lovely girl, stamping her tiny foot on the wet gravel. "But I'll keep your disgraceful secret as long as you never open your lips to me again. Do you hear?" angrily.

"I hear, and I'll stick to the condition, though it's a hard one. I had as soon be dead as banished from your presence," sighing. Then he looked at Beresford. "And you?" he said, anxiously.

"I'll never betray you unless you seek to harm Floy again in any way, even by speaking her name lightly, as you may in malice be tempted to do. You understand?" sternly.

"Yes, and I'll not forget that you have constituted yourself her protector."

There was a furtive sneer under the pretended humility of the answer, but Beresford did not heed it, he merely said, warningly: "See that you keep your promise," and turned away, going down the path with Floy at his side and out at the gate with her to the waiting carriage.

The craven wretch they had left behind followed more slowly, for he was indeed sore and bruised from his fall, and his ankle was twisted from his efforts to alight on his feet.

But as he had come afoot on his secret nefarious mission of evil, he was compelled to return the same way, cursing and groaning at every step with blended pain and chagrin, for his heart was filled with rage against Beresford.

"Curse him! He foiled my clever plan entirely!" he raved to himself.

9

BERESFORD LED HIS trembling young companion out to the carriage that waited impatiently at the gates, the horses fretting and the driver swearing under his breath.

In fact, the young man had been charged a heavy sum for this service, the driver sharing to the full the common terror of Suicide Place.

So it was with a sigh of relief that he received from Floy the directions where to drive, after which she was handed into the carriage by her escort.

"With your permission I will see you safely home," he said, courteously, springing in after her and closing the door.

They had something more than three miles to drive to Bird's Nest Cottage, and each heart thrilled with the consciousness of happy moments to be spent together.

As he seated himself by her side, Floy thought of her exquisite dream of the rose garden, where she had walked by his side, with his arm about her waist and his low voice whispering love into her willing and enraptured ears.

Her heart began to throb wildly, the blood leaped warmly through her veins, she felt her cheeks flush and her eyelids quiver in the semi-darkness. She was so overcome with sweet and painful emotion that she could not utter a word, and Beresford, thrilling with the same sweet pain, also remained silent.

He was so madly in love with the little blue-eyed beauty by his side that it was with difficulty he restrained himself from clasping the dainty form in his arms and whispering to her all that was in his heart—the admiration, the tenderness, the passion, the yearning to woo and win her for his worshiped bride.

But the faint remnant of reason remaining to him whispered, warningly:

"Wait till she knows you better. Such impetuous violence would frighten and disgust the little darling!"

So each remained silent for a brief time, thrilled and dominated by the presence of the other, then Floy, coming back to herself by a great effort of will, murmured, softly:

"You said you came to take me home. Did anyone send you?"

"No, I came of my own free will," he returned, gently.

"Why—why, that was strange!" she faltered, wonderingly.

"Do you think so?" he asked, and there was a tender meaning in his voice that made her cheeks burn warmly, and her heart throb again so wildly that she could not speak. She, who had always been so saucy and ready-witted, flouting with scorn the flatteries of her admirers, could not think of any retort, could not unclose her lips for a coquettish reply.

Finding that she did not reply, her handsome companion continued:

"I wonder if you would be offended if I should tell you about a strange dream that warned me to come to your assistance!"

Floy started and thrilled, remembering her own beautiful dream, and she found courage to return:

"I—I thought you were too much offended with me to—to dream of me! Otho said you were so angry with me, you would not come back to the picnic."

"That was not true. I was a little vexed with you, I own, but I was going back with Otho, only just as we stepped outside the gate, a telegram was handed me that necessitated my return to New York tomorrow, and my sailing for Europe the next day. The matter so worried me that I told Otho to go back without me, as I must remain to see to my packing. I did not bring my valet here with me, and he went alone and made capital of my absence to tell you that falsehood, the villain!"

"Oh, how I hate the false, cowardly wretch, and how glad I am that you came when you did. I believe I should have died with disgust if he had succeeded in kissing me!" cried Floy.

Beresford wondered if she would be willing to kiss him, but he did not dare to offer the caress that was burning on his lips. His strong, true love made him timid and respectful.

He said, soothingly:

"I do not think he will ever dare to annoy you again."

"I should think not, or I will tell Uncle John, and he will punish him," Floy replied, then added, timidly: "But the dream that sent you to me? —I am quite curious over it."

"I should like you to hear it, only—promise me you will not be angry," tenderly.

"Of course not. One cannot stop dreams. And this one must have been a good one."

"It was charming!" he cried, vivaciously.

"Then tell me all about it." And it seemed to him that all unconsciously to herself she nestled confidingly closer to his side.

He also leaned nearer, so that their heads were very, very close, so close that his warm breath ruffled the strands of her curly hair and swept her cheek, as he began:

"In the first place, I was seriously annoyed yesterday when I heard you answer Miss Maury's challenge, by declaring that you would spend the night alone in the haunted house—I believe it is said to be haunted, is it not? Although I was almost a stranger to you, and you seemed to avoid me somehow, I determined to seek an opportunity to dissuade you from your purpose, and to tell you frankly how imprudent such an adventure would be. I even determined that if you refused to listen to me I would seek out your parents and acquaint them with your girlish folly."

"But I have no parents—only adopted ones, you know."

"Yes, I heard the story of your life today from a young man who seemed to admire you very much," returned Beresford, adding: "But of course that made no difference, as your adopted parents would exercise the same authority over you as your own."

Floy remained demurely silent, smiling to herself at the thought of how those dear adopted parents always humored her every madcap whim.

"Said Brier-Rose's mother to the naughty Brier-Rose:
'Whatever will become of you the Lord Almighty knows!
You will not scrub the kettles, and you will not touch the broom,
You never sit a minute still at spinning-wheel or loom!'
"And oft the maiden cried when Brier-Rose went by:
'You cannot knit a stocking, you cannot make a pie!'
But Brier-Rose, as was her wont, she cocked a curly head,
'But I can sing a pretty song,' full merrily she said."

"But," continued the speaker, "after that came your sensational plunge into the water, frightening everyone out of their wits. When the funny farce of saving you was over, and I went back for dry clothes, that telegram drove everything else out of my mind for a while—even *you*," tenderly.

Floy did not answer a word. She listened attentively, thinking how sweet and musical his voice sounded, and how sorry she was that this charming drive would soon be over. She could have gone on, and on, and on with him forever.

But the cross driver, not sharing her predilections, swore at his horses and whipped them up impatiently, while Beresford added:

"The telegram drove everything else out of my mind until I retired, when I fell asleep and dreamed of you."

10

"*I DREAMED OF* you," repeated Beresford, bending lower over the girl until her fragrant breath floated up to him, and the magnetism of her nearness enveloped him in an atmosphere of passionate bliss. "I dreamed, little Floy, that you and I were alone together, walking in the most beautiful rose garden in the world."

"Oh!" cried Floy, with a delicious start, throwing up her little hands.

Beresford caught one of them in his and held it tenderly, as if it had been a little trembling white bird, as he went on softly:

"Words are too weak to describe the beauties of that spot."

"I can imagine it," thought Floy, recalling her own dream of roses.

"It must have been in Italy, the sky was so deeply blue, and the roses so grand," resumed Beresford. "There were thickets of roses so dense that the sun's rays had not dried the morning dew sparkling on their petals. There were winding walks bordered with rose trees; there were shady bowers wreathed with climbing roses; there were roses on the ground, roses in your hair—white ones— and at the waist of your white gown were pink and white ones blended."

"Oh-h-h!" breathed Floy, lost in wonder at the similarity of their dreams, and she listened breathlessly as he went on telling her how the far-off sound of the sea had come to his ears, mixed with the music that breathed of love—the same music she had heard in her own dream.

"Oh, how strange, how passing strange!" she sighed and he answered, tenderly:

"Yes, strange, but sweet, for now I come to the best part of it. And you must not be offended, Floy—remember, you said you would not—for in my dream we were lovers—you and I—and as

I walked, my arm was around your slender waist, you raised your face to mine, I kissed it, and called you my love, my bride."

One moment of thrilling silence, in which they could almost hear each other's wild hearts leap with joy, then Floy cried, eagerly:

"Oh, let me finish the dream for you! Did not a terrific storm arise and frighten me so that I cried out to you to save me? Did not a dark, beautiful woman rush in and thrust us apart?"

"Yes, oh, yes! that was how it ended. How strange that you should guess at so much of my dream, Floy! But that was the way of it. You clung to me, begging me to save you, and I assured you that I would, and just then a beautiful woman—she had the very face of Maybelle Maury—rushed in and thrust us apart with wild, jealous threats. At that moment I awoke in a cold perspiration, trembling with alarm, and the memory of you rushed over me, and I thought of you alone in that old house so horror-haunted, and your voice seemed calling for me to save you, until I sprung up, threw on my clothes, and darted from the room, intending to ask Maury to accompany me and take you away from that dreadful place."

"Yes?" breathed Floy, eagerly, as he paused.

"Well, I met Maury's manservant in the hall, and on asking for Otho, was told he had gone out. The man begged me to follow and bring him back, as he had been drinking again against his father's commands, and if it came to the old man's ears there would be a terrible row. He added that Otho had boasted he was going out to keep an engagement with a lady, but he suspected he might be found at some gambling hell, as he often frequented such resorts.

"'I will bring him back,' I assured the man, and rushed from the house, goaded by a frantic suspicion, hurried to a livery stable through the raging storm, secured the carriage after a long argument, and reached Suicide Place soon after the cessation of the storm. You know all that followed. I followed the light in the window, and secreted myself in the shrubbery just in time to witness the entrance of Maury. I heard all that passed between you, clambered over the sill, and collared the wretch just in the nick of time."

"Just in the nick of time!" echoed Floy, and she added, in a murmur, to herself: "Oh, that blessed dream that sent him to save me!"

He caught the whisper, and repeated, joyously:

"Yes, that blessed dream, for Heaven must have sent it to my pillow, forewarning me in dreams of your peril, that I might hasten to save you. But Floy—forgive me for calling you that so boldly, but it seems *so* natural——how strange it seems that you could follow my dream in thoughts as you did. You must possess the gift of mind-reading."

"No," she answered, hesitatingly, then burst out, solemnly: "Oh, it's so strange I can hardly tell you, and perhaps you will not believe me, but—I knew all your dream as soon as you began to relate it. For—this is the truth, sir, and not a girlish jest—tonight I fell asleep on the porch of Suicide Place before I came into the house, and dreamed the self-same dream just as you have told it, word for word."

She paused, awed and trembling, overcome by the strange co-incidence of her dream.

She heard George Beresford laugh low and joyously to himself. She felt him crush the hand he held against his throbbing heart, then he whispered, tenderly:

"Oh, happy, happy dream that brought us together! Let me interpret it, darling little Floy. It means that we indeed are lovers, that Heaven made us for each other. Do you not believe it?"

WHAT FLOY WOULD have answered to her lover's ardent question was lost in the rumble and noise of the carriage wheels as the driver reined up his horses in front of Bird's Nest Cottage, and loudly announced:

"Here we are!"

Beresford handed Floy out, and walked through the cottage gate up to the door with her, whispering under the leafy shade of the honeysuckle vines a tremulous question:

"Will you give me love for love, darling Floy? Will you marry me?"

She tried to draw away the hand he held, murmuring, agitatedly:

"You—you have no right to talk to me like this. You are engaged to Maybelle."

Her voice broke in a sob, and he put his arm around her, drawing her close to his side, hoping that the shadow of the vines was dense enough to prevent the inquisitive driver from watching their lovemaking.

"I'm *not* engaged to Maybelle. Never *was*, either. What made you think so, my sweet one?" he whispered.

"Otho Maury told me so the night before the picnic. He said you were to marry his sister in the fall."

"I'll be shot if I do! That is another of Otho's lies, my pet. The wish was father to the statement. But I never thought of marrying Maybelle, and they know it. You are my only sweetheart, dearest, and unless you promise to marry me, I shall sail the seas over with a broken heart tomorrow."

"Oh!" she sighed, doubtfully.

"It's true, dearest, and you must answer me quickly, for that driver is getting impatient, don't you know? And I cannot come back for an answer tomorrow, for I'll be on my way to New York before your blue eyes see the light in the morning, and the day after I sail for Europe, to be absent, at the shortest possible time, a month. And you won't be so cruel as to send me away in despair?"

She had always thought, in her maidenly dreams of love, that she should not answer yes to her lover's first proposal, she would keep him in suspense awhile, but at the thought of the long sea voyage, her tender heart quaked. What if he should be drowned, her darling boy, and never know she loved him so dearly?

"Answer me," he pleaded, and she sighed:

"It is so sudden."

Beresford laughed low and happily.

"Yes, Love was born full grown, was he not? Love at first sight, and it is delicious so. Oh, Floy, is it hopeless? Don't you love me just a little after all?"

"Not a little—a whole world full," she whispered, carried out of herself by his passion.

Just then the gruff driver bawled irascibly:

"Ain't you never coming, sir? It'll soon be daylight!"

Beresford caught her in his arms, pressing her tightly to his heart, as he whispered:

"You hear that impatient wretch! I must leave you, darling, but I shall be back in a month, and I'll write you while I'm gone. Wear this ring, but keep our sweet secret till I give you leave to speak. I must conciliate my little world first, you know. One kiss, darling, and don't forget your absent boy."

He kissed the sweet lips a dozen times, and felt her tears raining down her cheeks till they mixed their salty taste with the sweetness of her mouth. She could not speak one word more after her sweet impulsive avowal of her love, only trembled in his arms, with tears in her eyes and smiles on her lips, like April weather, till he snatched one last passionate kiss, and tore himself away.

Floy dashed the tears from her eyes and listened sadly to the carriage wheels as they rolled away, then turning back to the cottage door, knocked loudly for admittance.

12

PRETTY SOON JOHN Banks, in an old frayed dressing-gown, opened the door himself, exclaiming:

"I thought you were going to stay all night with the girls, dearie!"

"I changed my mind," she answered, softly, then threw her arms around his neck, laughing, and whispering: "I'm sorry I disturbed your nap, you dear old darling, but I'll creep softly up to my room, and you can go to sleep again directly, can't you?"

"Yes, I hope so, but I've not slept well tonight. My head aches a little. Maybe it will be all right in the morning. I'm glad you came home tonight, dear, I always feel better when you are in the house."

"Do you, Uncle John? Oh, how good of you, when I'm nothing but a care to you, after all—a care and expense!"

"Don't get such notions in your head, Floy. I love to work for you, that is what I told Miss Maury last evening, when she called to offer me a place for you in her father's great New York store. I told her you should never go while I lived to take care of you, my child. But she said you had almost promised to go. Did you?"

"No, not unless you were to drive me away, you dear old darling! No, I shall never leave you till I am—married—no, not even then, for I shall marry rich, and take you and auntie to live with me in my grand New York home."

"Castles in Spain!" laughed John Banks, incredulously, but it warmed his fifty-year-old heart to hear her gracious promises, and to realize how she loved him. He kissed her a fond good-night, and went back to his couch, where he slept better the few hours before the early dawn for knowing that his lovely adopted child, the merry madcap girl, was safe under the cottage roof.

And Floy, as she flew up the steps to her simple room, felt her heart throb with repentance over the way she had deceived the kind, trusting old soul, and resolved to make a clean breast of it in the morning by confessing her sojourn at Suicide Place.

"And I'll promise him to never, never, never, set my foot there again!" she vowed, shuddering at the thought of all she had endured that night.

"What a terrible night, and what a happy ending!" she murmured as she sunk among the downy pillows of her little bed, with her thoughts full of her lover, grand, noble George Beresford.

She could hardly realize her happiness, pretty little Floy, for only two days ago she had not seen his face, although now it was the star of her future.

Her head was so full of the events of the night, that it was a long time before she fell asleep, so she was left undisturbed in the early morning when Mrs. Banks prepared her husband's early breakfast and sent him off cheerfully to his work on a building two blocks away.

"Don't call her till she wakes of herself, Mary," he said as he kissed his wife good-bye and went away whistling merrily, though his head was not quite easy of its strange pain.

So Floy slept on deeply and dreamlessly like a weary child till the sun was several hours high in the heavens and the merry birds twittered unheard in the tree at her window—slept on sweetly, to wake at last in a confused haste with a terrible sense of disaster.

"Oh, what is the matter?" she shrieked aloud in fear and grief, springing up and rushing to the door.

For she had been startled from her calm, sweet sleep by the unwonted sounds of heavy footsteps lumbering in at the front door, while over all rose shrill, agonized cries in a woman's voice—cries of bitter bereavement.

13

FLOY STOOD SCARED and trembling at the head of the stairs, trying to make out what was going on below.

She presently recognized that it was the voice of Mrs. Banks, uplifted in those grievous cries, and a conviction of the truth rushed over her mind—something terrible had happened to John Banks.

The tender-hearted wife had always been nervous over his trade of house-builder—always forebode an accident.

Tears rushed blindingly to Floy's sweet blue eyes, and her heart sunk heavily as she thought:

"Poor, poor auntie! Her life-long presentiments are realized at last."

For what else could be meant by those heavy, lumbering steps down-stairs, and those doleful cries in the little house that was usually so calm and peaceful?

She groped with ice-cold fingers for a loose wrapper, threw it over her snowy night-gown, and thrusting her little rosy bare feet into tiny slippers, flew down the stairs.

The little front room seemed full of people.

There were men in working garb, without their coats, and homely neighbor women with their aprons to their eyes. There was *something* covered up solemnly on a couch, and beside it Mrs. Banks was kneeling, wringing her hands and filling their sorrowing ears with her doleful cries.

Floy rushed to the couch, but an old woman caught and held her back.

"It is Uncle John—I know it! Do not tell me he is dead!" she moaned.

But it was, alas! too true.

He had fallen from a scaffolding on the third story, and death had been instantaneous. The true and tender heart had ceased to beat, the noble nature had passed from earth to its reward in heaven.

"It was that dizziness in his head made him miss his footing. I know it. I begged him to stay at home till he was better, but he said they could not spare him, and now he is gone from me forever!" wailed the stricken widow.

And by the couch of death she and Floy mingled their anguished tears together, both so bitterly bereaved of their loved one and their only supporter.

For when the first days of grief had passed, and their dead had been laid away to rest in the graveyard beneath the sweet spring flowers, these two, the lonely woman and the helpless girl, had to look the future in the face.

The faithful hands that had toiled for them, the loving heart that had shielded them, these, alas! were no more, and grim poverty stalked into the little cottage now, a guest they could not thrust away.

The carpenter had worked faithfully all his life, but his meager savings had all been swept away by the failure of a savings bank to which he had trusted them. During the last two years of financial panic and stress he had been much out of work, and lately he had just caught up with the rents again, and given his wife and Floy their simple spring outfits.

There was nothing, nothing for them to look to but the labor of their hands. Poor Floy did not know how to do anything useful, they had spoiled and petted her so, and Mrs. Banks, who did plain sewing for the neighbors sometimes, knew that all her profits would not pay the cottage rent.

When the funeral expenses had been paid out of the money for her husband's last job, there remained to the poor woman only the simple furniture of the tiny cottage and five dollars in her purse.

"What are we to do?" she sobbed, pitifully.

It was then that Maybelle Maury came to the rescue.

"Mamma will employ you in her house as a seamstress, and papa will give Floy a place as salesgirl," said the dark-eyed beauty, cheerfully.

"Oh, I cannot be parted from my child!" exclaimed the unhappy widow, tearfully.

Maybelle curled an imperious lip, and answered:

"That is nonsense! You cannot keep Floy with you now. She will have to earn her living like other poor girls!"

Floy, sitting over at the window in dreary silence, thought, exultantly:

"Wait till my lover comes back from Europe, Maybelle, and see! Oh, it will break your proud heart when George Beresford marries me! And how he will laugh when I tell him of her grand airs now!"

She longed to startle Maybelle now by telling her that she would have no need to work for her living, that she was soon to marry a millionaire's son, and could take care of Mrs. Banks in luxury, but she remembered that Beresford had told her not to betray their secret till he gave her leave, because he must first propitiate his own little world. So she kept back the words, and at last said, with a careless little air that angered Maybelle deeply:

"We may as well accept these positions now, dearest auntie, and try to bear the separation as best we can for a while, but after I am married, and that may be before long, you shall come and live in my new home, and we shall be as happy as possible without our dear lost one!"

She could not forbear this little boast in her resentment against proud Maybelle, and the beauty looked at her angrily while Mrs. Banks exclaimed in smiling astonishment:

"Married—married! Why, who ever put such a notion in that little giddy head? Who would marry a child like you?"

"A child, auntie? Why, I was seventeen the day before the picnic, so I'll be eighteen my very next birthday, and many a girl is married before eighteen. Why, I may be engaged already for all you know to the contrary—although I don't swear that I am!" concluded Floy, fearing she had said too much, and not intending to arouse their suspicions.

But Maybelle, who knew from Otho all that had happened at Suicide Place the night when his dastardly plans had been foiled by Beresford's timely appearance, trembled with inward rage and fear, suspecting Floy's thinly veiled meaning.

Otho had left no stone unturned to find out all that had happened to Floy after Beresford took her away that night.

The carriage-driver had been ferreted out and interviewed, although he had nothing to tell except that he had driven the pair to

Bird's Nest Cottage as fast as he could, and that they had lingered and parted at the door like lovers, with a kiss.

In the story of that kiss all was told.

Otho knew that George Beresford, unlike the generality of rich young men, was a man of honor.

No young girl's ruin lay at his door.

He might flirt in a careless, non-committal way if invited to it by a pair of bold eyes, but he never trespassed the proprieties.

Maybelle had led him on as far as any, for she was one of the most accomplished coquettes of the day, but his bearded lips had never pressed the bloom from her lips and cheeks. If languishing eyes had dared and tempted him to the feast, he had most successfully resisted the temptation.

So Otho and his sister, knowing Beresford's honor and Floy's purity, knew full well the meaning of that kiss.

It was the sacred pledge of their solemn betrothal.

Ay, though they had known each other scarcely twenty-four hours, they had instantly recognized each other as soulmates. Their hearts had leaped together and melted into one beneath the burning sun of Love.

"When Love, like a red rose, burns and blushes,
How sweet is the kiss that warm lips give;
The soul's far deep at its coming hushes
The thirsting passions that in them live."

Otho, mad with love for Floy, and Maybelle for Beresford, knew that something terrible indeed must happen if these two were to be prevented from marrying.

Nothing short of Floy's death or dishonor would keep the proud young aristocrat from making her his worshipful bride.

Maybelle, in the madness of her jealous love, hated Floy with a terrible hate.

She felt that she had come very near to winning Beresford's love just before he met Floy.

And she vainly imagined that with Floy removed from her path, she might yet succeed in her heart's desire.

Love, ambition, and jealousy combined had transformed Maybelle from a merely selfish, domineering girl into a relentless fiend. She felt as if she would like to murder innocent Floy with her laughing blue eyes, and her saucy, winning smile so frank and ready. Why should this girl, socially her inferior, and with only a babyish kind of beauty, have won in one brief, fateful day the prize that Maybelle had schemed for long, weary months, and which she would have sold her soul to win?

When she thought of Floy's possessing Beresford for her very own, of the love and caresses she craved being lavished on the little beauty, she felt as if her heart leaped into her throat and choked her. She grew lividly pale with emotion.

She could not speak for a moment after Floy's little boast, and the young girl continued, lightly:

"But, auntie, we needn't really be parted at all. Why can't we go and live together at Suicide Place? It's mine, you know, and much grander, after all, than Bird's Nest Cottage. There is plenty of nice, old-fashioned furniture too, and I'm sure we could be comfortable. What do you say?"

But Mrs. Banks almost fainted at the bare idea.

"Oh, my pet, I'd make any sacrifice in the world for you, except that one!" she cried, in horror, and so Floy fell into the meshes of her hungry fate.

14

MRS. BANKS WAS wretched at the thought of being parted from Floy, whom she loved as dearly as if she had been her own child.

Tears sprung to her eyes, and she cried piteously:

"Oh, Maybelle, how can I let my child go into that great wicked city of New York, with all its terrible temptations to a poor girl who has to earn her bread! Couldn't I go, too, and watch over her young life?"

"How could you go? Floy will only earn five dollars a week, and that will barely provide her board, lodging, carfare, and clothing," answered Maybelle.

"Good heavens! I should say not," cried Mrs. Banks, in dismay. "But, oh, I did not mean to live on Floy's small earnings. Couldn't I get work in the city, too? If we had only one little room together, we could be happier than apart."

"Yes, I should not mind it so much if only you could be with me, dear," added Floy, eagerly.

But Maybelle was relentless.

The success of the plot she had in her mind depended on the separation of these two, who seemed to have no one in the world but each other.

So she persisted in throwing cold water on all the woman's plans, declaring that there were thousands of women out of work and starving in the great city, and that her father was doing Floy a great favor in giving her this position when hundreds of others would have been so glad to get it.

"And mamma can recommend Floy to a good lodging-house," she added. "It is kept by a woman who used to keep house for us when I was a child. She married a car-driver, and went to live in New York. She has been keeping a salesgirls' boarding-house ten years, and they have a charming home with her, I am sure. So Floy will be as safe with her as under your own protection."

"And you think she is a good woman, and will be kind to my poor child, Maybelle?"

"Yes, indeed!" earnestly.

"That takes a load off my mind, I assure you, and I will write this woman a special letter, or perhaps I had better go with Floy to New York myself and talk with this Mrs. —"

"Horton," said Maybelle.

"Yes, Horton—thank you."

"Very well—if you can spare the money for the trip—although a letter would do just as well, and papa would take Floy to New York with him any morning and put her in the woman's care."

"Do you think he would be so kind?" exclaimed Mrs. Banks, reminded by Maybelle's hints of her scarcity of money, and thinking that she had better save what she had for a little nest-egg for Floy to take with her in case of sickness or other needs, for her salary would be such a miserable pittance.

In the end, Maybelle persuaded her to send Mrs. Horton a letter instead of going to New York herself, so at parting with Floy she pressed the five-dollar bill into the girl's hand, whispering tenderly:

"You may need it, dear."

Floy thrust it back, crying out:

"It is your little all, I cannot take it!"

"Yes, you must, my darling, for I shall have more from the sale of the furniture, you know."

Floy kept it reluctantly. She vowed that she never would use it except in case of direst need.

And so with tears in her eyes, and her sweet bright face clouded with trouble, she parted from the good woman who had been like a mother to her for almost ten years, and went her way to the city with Mr. Maury, who was acting in good faith toward the girl, and did not dream that his son and daughter, in begging him to give Floy a place in his store, were only using him as a tool to further the nefarious designs they had against the poor girl's happiness.

But the pair of plotters were in haste to get in their cruel work, for they knew that George Beresford did not expect to remain away more than a month.

In that month they must accomplish the task they had set themselves—to build a wall between Floy and Beresford too high for either to scale, in short, to make that parting at the cottage door an eternal separation.

Maybelle had called at the cottage with her father to see Floy off, and when the parting was over she turned to the sobbing Mrs. Banks, and asked, curiously:

"What was it that she ran back to whisper to you at the last moment?"

Mrs. Banks did not dream how much was involved in her answer. She thought it a matter of little moment, and answered, carelessly:

"She told me that if any letters came for her to Mount Vernon to send them to her at once in New York."

"So she has a correspondent?" Maybelle muttered, jealously.

"Why, no, indeed, miss, I don't believe the child ever received a letter in her whole life. I think she must have meant it for fun, for who would write her a letter? She has no relations that she knows of, and no real friend but me, poor little one!"

"Perhaps she has a clandestine love affair."

"No, indeed, Maybelle, I'm sure not. She was only joking."

"Well, Mrs. Banks, I must go now. Shall I tell mamma that you will come tomorrow?"

"If you please, miss, for I shall get things ready to have the auction sale of my household effects in the morning."

Maybelle hurried away, and her next interview was with the letter-carrier for that district.

She told him that Florence Fane had gone to New York to live, and had requested her—Maybelle Maury—to receive any letters that might come to her address. He was to deliver them privately to her keeping, that her aunt might not discover the correspondence she was carrying on.

The carrier promised compliance.

15

FLOY WAS TAKEN to Mr. Maury's palatial store, on one of the most prosperous business thoroughfares of New York, and given a position behind the handkerchief counter.

Her genial, sunny nature, always looking at the bright side of everything, soon attracted admiring friends among her fellow employees, and made her popular with the elegant customers who patronized the well-known importing house.

She was so frank, so pretty, so engaging that it was a pleasure to be waited on by such a girl, who, while eager to please, did not feel abashed by the notice of the stately ladies of the grand Four Hundred, nor permit herself to be patronized by them. She had a rare and graceful dignity, this wild rose of a girl, that repelled insolence and patronage alike. When her fellow salesgirls twitted her on her air of easy independence, declaring that it would give offense, she tossed her shining head and answered, saucily:

"Why, I am as good as they are, so why should I cringe to them? Money is the only difference between us."

They laughed at her, but in their hearts they admired her independence, and they said among themselves that there was not a rich girl who came to the store half as pretty and dainty as merry little Floy, in her cheap blue dress that set off to such advantage her flower-like face, and tiny dimpled hands with their exquisite taper fingers.

Floy would not own even to herself that she really occupied a very subordinate position in the world, for there was some proud blood in her veins that made her hold her little head high, and, besides, didn't she know in her heart that she was engaged to the son of a millionaire—the dearest fellow in the world, too, who was coming back in a month to claim her for his happy bride?

She said to herself blithely enough that this selling handkerchiefs across a counter was only an episode in her life, brought about by the jealous malice of Maybelle Maury, and that it would soon be over forever. Next year she would be coming to Maury & Co.'s in her own liveried carriage to buy the costly handkerchiefs of web-lace and fine embroidery. How the girls she worked with now would stare and nudge each other with surprise when she appeared!

She had a foretaste of this one day when a beautiful, brown-eyed woman sailed up to the counter and set all the clerks whispering to each other.

How grand she was, how stately! and her gray gown was a Parisian importation—all the girls knew that, even Floy, though she had been in New York barely a week.

The lady asked for lace handkerchiefs in a musical voice that made Floy's heart leap wildly, while the frankly admiring brown eyes made her blush like a wild rose. The voice and the eyes were so like—so like those that Floy dreamed of every night.

She was a little nervous while she displayed the beautiful handkerchiefs. Some of the girls noticed it, and they whispered to one another that Floy was losing some of her saucy independence, and was overawed at last by a Fifth Avenue swell.

The lady was very kind and gracious, and she looked admiringly at the lovely salesgirl while she counted out the money—something over a hundred dollars—to pay for the dainty trifles she had purchased. As she was turning away, she said:

"Send the package to Mrs. Beresford, No. — Fifth Avenue."

Then Floy comprehended instantly that the handsome, gracious lady was none other than George Beresford's mother.

She gazed after her almost yearningly till she had passed through the street door, then turned to replace the boxes of handkerchiefs on the shelves.

And as she did so, she noticed that the lady had carelessly left her well-filled purse on the counter under a drift of snowy lawn.

"Oh!" she cried, breathlessly, catching it up and rushing in swift pursuit.

The footman was just opening the carriage door for his lady when Floy appeared, her sweet face like a rose, her hair a tangle of gold in the sunshine.

"Madame—Mrs. Beresford—your purse! You left it on the counter!" she cried, incoherently.

"Thank you very much, my dear," answered the lady, turning and taking the purse, and the girl's hand with it. Gazing admiringly at Floy, she laughed sweetly, and exclaimed: "Do you know how I chanced to forget it? You are so very pretty, I kept staring at you as if you were a picture until the purse must have dropped unconsciously from my hand. It was very good of you to run after me with it, and I shall reward you with some of the contents."

And she was opening the dainty gold-mounted *porte-monnaie*, when Floy's little hand closed it impetuously.

"No, no, you must not—I cannot accept it!" she exclaimed, confusedly, but with a little imperious air that bespoke secret indignation, and with a courteous bow to the surprised lady, she hurried back into the store.

Mrs. Beresford entered her carriage, feeling somehow as if she had been gently snubbed, and saying to herself, half smiling:

"The saucy little thing! I should have thought she would be glad to get five dollars so easily. I should have liked to reward her for her honesty, too, for some girls would have been mean enough to keep the purse. There's five hundred dollars in it, too, that I brought out to spend on a bridal gift for Cousin Marion. But that girl, so lovely and dainty, made me forget everything. She's proud enough and pretty enough for a princess, and it's a pity she's poor, for beauty is too often a curse to a poor salesgirl."

When Floy ran back to finish putting away the handkerchief boxes, several curious girls hastened to help her and to congratulate her on having made such a handsome sale to Mrs. Beresford.

"She's as rich as cream and peaches—her husband has so many millions he can't count 'em," declared one, rashly.

"Her house is a marble palace on Fifth Avenue. We will go out with you to see it Sunday, if you like."

"Didn't she make you a present for returning her purse?" queried another curious one.

"Certainly not," Floy answered, proudly.

"She wouldn't take it. I saw her push Mrs. Beresford's purse back with so queenly an air that the lady stared with surprise," laughed Nell Jarley.

The girls all made great eyes of wonder, and one said that Floy should have taken the reward.

Floy only listened, and smiled like one in a sweet waking dream. She was charmed with the gracious beauty of her lover's mother, and she thought, with tender pride:

"When I am his wife I will create as much sensation as she does when she comes here to shop."

And just then one of her mates said, carelessly:

"With all that money, the Beresfords have only two children, a son and daughter, to inherit it."

"Is—is—the son married?" asked Floy, timidly, and they all laughed.

"What a question! Are you thinking of setting your cap for him, princess! No, he is not married yet, though they do say he has fallen in love with Mr. Maury's eldest daughter. She is very lovely and stylish, and comes here often. George Beresford comes here, too, with his mother now and then. He is perfectly splendid."

Floy wondered, with a throbbing heart, what they would say if they knew that she was betrothed to this grand Beresford.

16

FLOY WENT HOME that evening from the store with a blithe heart.

The meeting with George Beresford's mother had been a delight to the innocent girl.

The great lady's graciousness had thrilled her with hope.

She remembered how anxiously her lover had admitted that he must conciliate his little world before his marriage.

It seemed to her simple mind that Mrs. Beresford had been won over already.

"She told me I was pretty—that she was looking at me as if I had been a picture. She cannot be angry with her son for loving me," she murmured, sagely, and she decided that if he should write her a letter from abroad she would answer it at once, telling him all that had happened since their parting and of her pleasant *rencontre* with his charming mother.

Dimpling with happy smiles, the fragment of a love-song on her rosy lips, Floy climbed the uncarpeted stairs to her own poor little den, away up under the eaves in the fourth story, where a minute later she was followed by her landlady, pudgy Mrs. Horton.

The woman carried in her hand a beautiful bunch of roses and a letter.

"These came for you a while ago, Floy," she said, blandly.

"From whom?" exclaimed Floy, in surprise.

"Some of your beaus, I suppose. Better read the letter and see," the woman returned good-naturedly.

Floy tore it open with nervous fingers, and read these words written in an elegant masculine hand:

"DEAR LITTLE FLOY—I cannot rest under the ban of your anger.

"We used to be such good friends before that night at Suicide Place that I think you might forgive my folly when I was so drunk I did not realize what I was doing—nothing worse, after all, than trying to steal a kiss from the sweetest lips in the world. Many a pretty girl has forgiven a little fault like that in an adoring lover.

"Ah, will you not forgive me and be friends again?

"I am coming to call on you this evening to take you to the Garden Theater if you will accompany me. The play is 'Trilby'— of course you've read that wonderful 'Trilby' that has made such a sensation—and I think you will enjoy it. Do not refuse, I beg of you.

"Be ready when I call—I send you some roses for you to wear—and I promise you a charming time.

"O. M.

"Union League Club, New York, May 21st, 1895."

Floy stood motionless and pale to the lips, gazing at the letter as if it had been a Gorgon's head and had turned her to stone.

"Oh, Floy, I hope it's not bad news!" cried the landlady.

Floy roused herself from her trance of indignation, and answered, angrily:

"Mrs. Horton, if a gentleman calls for me this evening you will kindly tell him I am not at home. As for these flowers, you may have them or throw them out of the window."

"Thank you kindly, miss," replied the woman, taking them down to ornament her stuffy little parlor.

And there Otho Maury found them when he made his call. He crushed an oath under his black mustache as he asked, eagerly:

"Is Floy at home?"

"Lor,' Mr. Maury, are you the one that sent her the flowers?"

"Yes," he replied, coldly.

"Oh, sir, I'm sorry to tell you, but she burned your letter and gave me the roses, and told me to say she was not at home!" blurted out Mrs. Horton, in her amazement at Floy's antagonism to this charming exquisite.

Otho repressed his rage, and said, gratingly:

"That's strange. Wonder how I have offended the young woman? She used to be awfully fond of me at Mount Vernon. There's some misunderstanding, and if I could see her one moment I know I could set it straight with the pretty little vixen. Mightn't I just go up and knock at her door?"

"I don't see as there'd be any *great* harm, sir. It's the fourth flight, No. 19."

Floy had forgotten to lock her door after Mrs. Horton went, she was so angrily intent on setting a match to Otho's letter.

"How dare he persecute me so?" she cried, with flashing eyes as she watched it shrivel to ashes.

The tea-bell rang, but she did not heed it. She was too excited to be conscious of hunger.

She lighted her lamp, bathed her hot face, brushed out her tangled curls, then raised the window and looked down into the street at the motley crowds beneath the glaring lights.

She was startled from a long reverie by the soft opening and closing of her door.

Turning about with a cry of alarm, Floy saw Otho Maury standing with his back against the door, an insolent smile of triumph on his lips.

"Floy, let me speak to you one moment," he pleaded humbly.

"No, I will not listen. How dare you come up here? Leave the room this instant, you villain!" she cried out in stormy anger.

"By Heaven, I will not go, you pretty little vixen, till you hear me. Oh, Floy, I love you. I offer you my heart and protection! Will you accept them? No! Then I swear I'll have the kiss you denied me that other night!"

Maddened with passion for the scornful young beauty, he advanced toward her, and in her terrible fright at the thought of his loathed caress, she leaned her slight body far over the sill, and sent her voice ringing down to the street in agonized shrieks:

"Help! help! help!"

"Oh, horror! horror!"

It was Otho who cried out then, for the girl suddenly lost her balance and plunged headlong through the window, going down, down, down, through the dizzy distance to a terrible death!

17

"*MY GOD, THE* girl will be instantly killed!" groaned Otho Maury, with blanched lips, and staggering like a drunken man as he reeled backwards to the door.

For even in the horror and remorse of the moment, knowing that he had caused Floy's death as certainly as though he had plunged a dagger in her heart, a swift, prudential consideration restrained him from following his first impulse to rush to the window and watch the doomed girl's terrible plunge to destruction.

"I must not be suspected of having caused her accident by my persecutions," he thought, in alarm for his reputation.

A blind impulse of flight seized upon him, and, trembling with horror, his face ashen white, his evil black eyes staring blankly before him, he made his exit from the room and the house without encountering anyone.

As he gained the street he heard a tumult of excited voices, but his guilty conscience would not permit him to join the crowd that was collecting on the pavement.

Wickedly as he had plotted against the poor girl's happiness, he felt that he could not bear the sight of her poor mutilated body with all the sweet, saucy beauty crushed out of the poor dead face.

If it were Maybelle now, she would gloat over the sight in her joy that her beautiful rival was dead.

But it was different with Otho, for deep in his heart burned a mad passion for bewitching Floy.

Though he had plotted with his sister to destroy her, it was her soul *he* meant to wreck, not her beautiful body. *That* he worshiped with doting admiration, and had hoped to win.

It almost seemed as if the hands of angels had been outstretched to foil his nefarious designs, and to draw Floy back, pure and unspotted, to heaven.

With these thoughts raging in his excited mind, Otho fled in horror from the scene, and to drown his haunting remorse, spent the night in a drunken orgy with some boon companions, who took him to his hotel in the "wee sma' hours ayant the twal," and consigned him to the porters to put to bed.

At noon of the next day he awoke with the usual large head incident to such dissipations, and swore at himself for a besotted fool, after which he ordered brandy and soda and breakfast.

When he had been bathed, and shaved, and dressed, he still remained pale, tremulous, and shaken, for the horror of last evening had rushed freshly over his mind.

"She is dead, poor little Floy, so pretty and so gay, like a merry little hummingbird ever on the wing—dead, and Maybelle will rejoice at the news, but as for me, I must ever bear about with me a load of remorse that will drive me to madness," he groaned, as he rang the bell for the morning papers, nerving himself to read an account of the tragedy.

It was there, on the first page of the paper they brought him, in glaring headlines:

"A PLUNGE TO DEATH!

"A Beautiful Young Girl Falls from the Fourth-Story Window of Her Home on Adams Street, and is Removed to Bellevue Hospital in a Dying Condition.

"As newsdealer Herr Spiel was dozing last evening in a chair by his news-stand on Adams Street, he was startled from his dreams by hearing something fall with a dull thud on the awning above his head, and springing to his feet, saw with consternation a beautiful young girl roll off the awning down to the pavement.

"At first sight the girl seemed to have escaped without injury after her fearful fall, for she rose to her feet very quickly, and stood looking about her with a half-shy smile, as if hoping that no one had noticed her accident.

"But in the next moment the pretty face grew pale, the smile faded, and with a groan she sunk unconscious to the earth.

"She was Miss Frances Fane, a boarder in the house, and had in some inexplicable manner fallen out of her window in the fourth story. She was removed to Bellevue Hospital in an unconscious condition, believed to be due to internal injuries, and will probably die."

Otho Maury read the paragraphs with working feature, for he knew that the victim was Floy, although a mistake had been made in her name, giving it as Frances.

"So she will die, poor little girl, poor little Fly-away Floy," he muttered, heavily. "Indeed, it is a marvel that she escaped instant death. Heigho! I must go home today, and carry the news to Maybelle."

And Otho swept his hand across his eyes to shut out the vision of a fair dead face that he had loved so well in its living beauty, so gay and sunny.

Then he remembered that Mrs. Vere de Vere had told him yesterday that Maybelle was coming to New York today. So he hurried to Fifth Avenue, and found her just arrived.

He drew her aside to tell her what had happened to Floy, and even his callous nature was shocked at her savage glee.

"What a cruel heart you have, Maybelle!" he cried in disgust.

She flashed him an angry look, and answered:

"I am no worse than you, Otho. Remember what a fate you plotted for the girl! She is better off as it is, for death is better than dishonor."

"A fine sentiment," he gibed, wondering if she thought herself quite honorable, as she had connived at the plot.

She read his thought, and tossed her head defiantly, thinking how glad she was that Floy was out of her way, by whatever means.

Otho sighed, and said:

"If you are going back to Mount Vernon tomorrow, perhaps you will break the news to Mrs. Banks? Poor soul!"

"No, I shall not go so soon. Besides, we need not hurry. Better wait till all is over. If she found out before Floy died, she would want to come down here and see her, and mamma could not really spare her now. She is busy with the summer sewing," Maybelle answered, heartlessly.

"I must be going," he said, with a tortured sigh, remorse heavy at his heart.

"No, stay, and go with us to the *matinée* to see 'Trilby.' Mrs. Vere de Vere has invited a little box party—the Van Dorns and the Beresfords. Join us, and you may get in a word with Alva Beresford."

"Hang Alva Beresford!" he replied, with the impatience of pain.

"Don't be a fool, Otho. You know you said you would help me catch George if I would perform a similar office for you with Alva."

"Yes, I know, but when did she get back from Paris and her painting?"

"Oh, weeks and weeks ago, and they say she has fitted up a magnificent studio at home and paints away all the time, as if she had to work for a living."

"Well, then, what's the use of my making up to such a girl? She has refused every fellow in society, I'm told. And she's getting quite a spinster—bachelor girl, I mean—isn't that the latest fad?"

"Alva is twenty-seven, that's a fact—nearly three years older than her brother—but she is still the most magnificent beauty in New York, and will have millions at her father's death. She is devoted to her daubing— 'wedded to her art,' she calls it—but she's only a woman after all, and some day she will lose her heart, of course. And why not to you, Otho, as well as another?" cried Maybelle, eagerly.

18

OTHO MAURY JOINED the theater party to see "Trilby," and devoted himself to the beautiful brown-eyed Alva Beresford, who looked like a young princess, and accepted his devotion with the careless patronage of one who knows that homage is her due.

It was her first meeting with Otho, and she read him at sight, and despised him accordingly, perhaps fathoming his designs on her fortune as she had already fathomed Maybelle's efforts to insnare George.

The Beresfords tolerated Maybelle without admiring her, and they were not pleased with the rumor that George was the young girl's suitor. They had higher views for the noble, handsome son of the house.

So perhaps it was with a spice of malice toward Maybelle that Alva said, gayly, in a pause between the acts:

"Do you see how sober mamma looks? She had a great fright this morning."

"Alva!" cried that lady, with a reproving nod, but her daughter, who was at times very volatile, laughed at her, and continued:

"She received her first letter from my brother, written on shipboard, and mailed at Queenstown. He perpetrated a terrible joke on mamma, declaring that he is in love at last."

She saw the hot color flame into Maybelle's cheeks, and continued, maliciously:

"George is contemplating a shocking *mésalliance*. He is in love, he says, with a pretty little nobody, poor as poverty, and wild as a deer. He intended to postpone his confession until his return a month hence, and beg our consent to his marriage, but his heart is so full he cannot wait. He begs mamma to write and give him some hope that she will approve his choice."

"Who is she?" Mrs. Vere de Vere inquired, trying to keep the blank look out of her face, her feelings stirred for Maybelle's sake.

"He did not tell us her name or home, much to mamma's regret, as if she only knew where to find her she would go and buy off her claims on George before he returns."

"Alva! Alva!" cried her mother, remonstratingly, but the daughter, who really regarded the whole affair as a huge joke of her brother, who seemed still but a boy to her maturer age, simply bubbled over with laughter, and continued:

"As it is, mamma is seriously contemplating an immediate trip across 'the pond' to persuade her boy out of his fancy, or to detain him abroad until his lovely charmer wearies of waiting his return and bestows her affections elsewhere."

At her light, merry tone everyone laughed, and Mrs. Van Dorn said, consolingly:

"I dare say it is only some pretty little actress, that he will forget in a week."

"I only hope so," sighed Mrs. Beresford, and then Mrs. Van Dorn, pitying her embarrassment, turned the conversation into other channels.

They talked of books and art, and now Mrs. Beresford could turn the tables on mischievous Alva.

"I shall punish Alva finely for telling my secret woes!" she exclaimed.

Everyone turned to her eagerly, and she continued:

"You see, Alva is painting a Cupid, but she cannot find a face to please her, and yesterday I saw a little salesgirl—in your father's store, by the way, Miss Maury—who had an ideal face for the picture. Such a face! all dimples and roses, blue eyes, and rings of golden hair on the graceful boyish head. And her smile—it was something to dream of were one a man—saucy, sweet, enchanting—such a smile as Cupid himself might wear when drawing his bow to transfix a heart. Well," drawing a long breath, "I meant to go tomorrow morning and secure this little beauty as a model for Alva's Cupid, but to punish her now I shall not do so, so the charming picture will never be painted."

"You cruel mamma, I shall go and find her myself tomorrow, and you will be balked of your revenge!" exclaimed Alva, with sparkling eyes, and for the rest of the time she could think of nothing but the lovely face she was going to secure for her Cupid.

Otho whispered to Maybelle:

"It must have been Floy that she saw at father's store."

"Yes," she answered, and exulted in her heart that the fair Cupid face had lost its roses, the blue eyes their happy light, the rosy mouth its witching smile, all faded in death.

Then the curtain raised again, and they turned to watch the mimic woes of "Trilby" and her lover.

Otho watched with dull, glazed eyes, that saw through all the glare and brightness the face of one lost to him forever, and when the actors recited the griefs of "Pauvre Trilby," his heart echoed "Pauvre Floy!"

19

IN THE LETTER that Alva Beresford treated as a merry jest, George had poured out the tenderness of a love-freighted heart to his mother.

When he parted from Floy that night beneath the vines on the cottage porch and hurried away to perform the mission on which he was sent across the sea, his heart was full of her grace and beauty, and every hour seemed leaden winged that kept him from her side.

"How beautiful she is, how far above all others in her ineffable grace and charm!" he said to himself every hour, and in his impatience to have her for his own he could not wait till his return to propitiate his mother, for whose sympathy he yearned with the eagerness of a loving son. He determined to write to her and plead his cause.

He knew, alas! all the Beresford pride, and how high it soared. Had not Alva's heart been crucified on its altar? —gay, mocking Alva, in whose past lay the story of a broken love-dream never to be resurrected now, for he was dead, the young poet lover whose suit her parents had scorned when Alva was a budding girl, fit incarnation of a poet's dream. It was only a few months later that he died—of a lingering fever, said the physicians—of a broken heart, vowed the girl, flinging it frantically in her parents' face in the desperation of her keen despair.

Well, the key was turned on that past. Few knew the story of its bitter pathos, but George recalled it now with something like terror—prophetic terror.

He cried to himself, resolutely:

"They shall not break my heart on the rack as they did poor Alva's. I am a strong man, she was only a weak girl. I will never give up my heart's love as she did, and drag out a cynical life, enjoying nothing, giving all my soul to cold, lifeless art in lieu of a broken love-dream. No, I shall marry pretty Floy, my heart's darling, and our life shall be ideally happy."

So he mused while pacing the steamer-deck the long starlit nights, and one day the letter was written to his mother, telling of his love, and begging for her approval.

Then he wrote to his little sweetheart—the first letter he had ever penned to her, and it was so full of his love and hope, that, had Floy received it, her heart would have thrilled for joy at the story it told—the story that blanched Maybelle's cheek with rage, for she, according to her plans, received Floy's letter from the postman, and ruthlessly broke the seal in the solitude of her chamber.

And how jealously her bosom throbbed, how ashen grew her cheek, as she read the burning words of love written to her innocent little rival, bonny Floy.

It seemed to her that a love so true as that expressed in those pages could never be turned aside from its object save by some fateful tragedy. Floy seemed to fill his heart to overflowing.

He left the ship at Queenstown, and posted his letters. Then, having attended to some business in Ireland, he crossed over to London to pursue his mission, counting in his heart every day and hour until he should receive answers from Floy and his mother, for he had begged them for immediate replies.

And every day he wrote again to Floy—love letters full of the tenderness that thrilled his heart:

"And so I write to you, and write, and write, and write,
For the mere sake of writing to you, dear.
What can I tell you that you know not?
Locked in my heart thou liest!
Love has set our souls in music to the self-same air."

A week passed, then another, and he knew the time had come when he might begin to look for letters if his correspondents were prompt.

It was now three weeks since he had left New York, but his hope of returning in a month was nipped in the bud.

The business on which his father had dispatched him dragged wearily along, and did not promise to turn out successfully. His lawyer said frankly that it would very likely detain him another month.

Just as he was beginning to chafe impatiently over the delay, came the anxiously awaited letter from his mother.

Oh! how eagerly he broke the seal, the color flying to his face, his heart beating like a trip-hammer.

For he longed for the approval of his family on his choice, longed for them to love and admire pretty Floy as he did, longed to take her to the great stately home where she would be like a glancing sunbeam in the grand surroundings.

He snatched the letter from its thick perfumed envelope, and his eager brown eyes glanced down the thickly written pages penned by the hand of his beautiful, proud mother.

How could she be so cruel to the boy she loved so dearly?

Had she forgotten the tortured heart of Alva, that she could doom her son to a like anguish?

Poor Alva—belle, beauty, and heiress—yet—*poor* Alva!

Whispering in her empty heart the name of one that died heart-broken for her sake!

Yes, the pride of birth and wealth that had stood between Alva and her happiness now threatened shipwreck also to her brother's bark of love.

Mrs. Beresford, in a passion of imperious anger, denounced the weakness and folly of her son.

She wrote, bitterly:

"You are a man, and of course I cannot forbid you from making the dreadful *mésalliance* you contemplate, but I can say positively, from your father and myself, that should you persist in your determination to wed this nobody—whose very name you were ashamed to mention—you will cut yourself off from our love and recognition, and also from inheriting one penny of the Beresford millions. As you have nothing to look to but the small legacy you had from your grandfather, perhaps this will bring you to your senses. Doubtless it will cure that scheming adventuress of her fancy for you—some second-rate actress, at the best, I suppose—and you had as well advise her of the change in your prospects should you follow your insane desire to marry such a creature! Our determination on this point is unalterable."

Every scathing word sunk deep into her son's heart, and with an inarticulate cry of anger and pain, he tore the offensive letter into ribbons, and cast it beneath his feet, trampling it as if it had been a living serpent.

"I might have known it!" he cried, bitterly. "They did not spare poor Alva, and they will not spare me! But I am not a child as my sister was. I will show them I am made of sterner stuff!"

He raged up and down the floor, his eyes blazing with insulted pride.

Though he had destroyed the letter, he could see in his mind's eye every offensive word standing out clearly, as though traced with a pen of fire.

He muttered in savage wrath, blended with wounded pride:

"Such cruel epithets— 'this nobody' — 'this scheming adventuress'— 'some second-rate actress' — 'such a creature' —oh, shame! that my lovely, innocent, pure-minded Floy should be insulted thus! Well, I will show them how I will come to my senses!"

He threw himself down at a table with his face on his arm, his broad shoulders heaving with emotion.

Long minutes passed while he fought the battle between filial duty and affection and the strong love of his life—strong and eternal, though such a short time ago he had not seen her face nor heard her name.

Love had passed over his soul like a torrent, bearing everything before it. To some deep natures love comes like this, and then it is either a tragedy of pain or a heaven of bliss.

Love scorns degrees. The low he lifteth high;
The high he draweth down to that fair plane
Whereon, in his divine equality,
Two loving hearts may meet.

Beresford lifted his head, his face transfigured with its passionate love and wounded pride.

Drawing a sheet of paper to him, he seized a pen, and wrote rapidly:

"May God forgive you, my beloved mother, for your cruel pride, and comfort you for the loss of your son, for you have forced me to choose between you and my heart's love. You have put my heart on the rack, like Alva's, but I am not weak like she was, my poor sister, so I, loving you still, and praying as ever for your welfare, renounce everything you choose to withhold from me, for my love's sake."

It was signed and posted, the brief letter, and then he realized the might of his love for Floy, that could reconcile him to such a renunciation as he had made.

He was no longer the heir of a millionaire, but a disinherited son, with nothing to live on but an income of three thousand a year left him by his grandfather. What then? He and Floy would be poor in gold, but rich in love. He could bear anything, so that she was not taken away from him.

Two days passed, and then there came another letter from New York. It was from Otho Maury—a smooth, fawning letter, pleading the paragraph he enclosed as an excuse for writing.

It was the story of poor little Floy's accident, and Otho wrote briefly of what had happened to Floy since Beresford had gone away—the death of John Banks, and Floy's venture as a salesgirl in New York, with the unaccountable accident that had closed the brief story of her sweet life, for at the end of the paragraph Otho penciled:

"*She died the next day.* Thinking you had a kindly interest in the sweet girl is the reason why I have written you," he added. "As for myself, I loved her, and had proposed marriage, but she refused me. I hope that our mutual admiration for the dear girl may form a bond of sympathy between us."

George Beresford could not bear the terrible shock of this letter, following on the excitement of his mother's denunciation.

His senses reeled before it, and he sunk in a heavy swoon to the floor, where an attendant discovered him presently and summoned a physician, who found him suffering from the first symptoms of brain fever.

Days and weeks of severe illness followed, but before he fell into a delirium he gave strict orders that no news of his condition should be sent to America.

20

THE DAY AFTER the theater party Miss Beresford stood alone in her beautiful studio in a sunny wing thrown out at the side of the mansion, and gazed meditatively at her latest work.

She was no mean artist, this queenly heiress, for having much talent in the beginning, she had improved upon it by spending several years in Paris under the best masters. She threw all her soul into her work, and delighted in every successful effort she made.

Her most ambitious work, and one that had occupied much time and study, was one that she called "Cupid."

It represented the beautiful little god of love strolling through a green wood, and coming suddenly on a party of lovely youths and maidens dancing on the banks of a crystal stream.

Cupid, charmed by the pretty sight, instantly determined to make himself two victims in the merry party. The picture represented Cupid, the mischievous little god, drawing his bow to transfix a heart with a piercing arrow.

One can fancy how sweet and arch and happy Cupid must have appeared at that moment when exercising his fateful power.

The large canvas was almost finished, and the painting was spirited and striking. The best judges could have found little fault in the execution. One more touch and it would be perfect.

The unfinished part was the face of Cupid.

Alva had despaired of putting on canvas the face of Cupid as it appeared to her fancy.

Beautiful faces she could find in plenty, but the arch, radiant smile, the laughing eyes so brightly blue, these eluded her brush.

"If I could only find a living face like my ideal and put it on canvas!" she cried, eagerly, over and over to her mother, who at last became almost as anxious over the subject as Alva herself.

It was no wonder that the lady had told Floy she had looked at her as at a beautiful picture, for in the young girl's enchanting face she had seen the realization of Alva's dream.

And the artist, standing before her unfinished work, recalled her mother's words of the day before, and cried out, joyously:

"I must find that lovely girl! She must be my model!"

Hastening to her mother, she exclaimed:

"You must come with me this morning to find Cupid!"

"Excuse me, Alva, but I cannot go today. I—I am not feeling well. Besides, I have just commenced a letter to your brother."

Alva did not ask what would be written to her brother. She could guess only too well by the thorn in her own heart.

She repressed a bursting sigh of sympathy for George, and said, determinedly:

"Then tell me where to find her, for I am going alone this very hour."

"She was a young salesgirl at the handkerchief counter at Maury & Co.'s. I bought those exquisite cobweb lace handkerchiefs from her, you know."

"Her name, mamma?"

"I did not ask it, Alva, but you cannot fail to know her, for there is no one like her. She is the loveliest salesgirl in New York, and looks like a princess."

"Tall or short, mamma?"

"Of medium height, dear, slenderly yet exquisitely formed, with a face of rarest beauty."

"It should be a boy's face, mamma."

"This one is boyish, Alva, because the sunny hair lies in soft loose rings of short hair all over the pretty head, and the roguish smile, and the dimples, the sea-shell coloring, the marvelous eyes so brightly blue, so innocent—arch—oh, I cannot describe them! —go see for yourself."

"I will, and you may expect me to bring her home with me."

She hurried out, ordered the carriage, and within an hour was on her way to the store.

Mrs. Beresford turned back with a sigh to her task, and finished the cruel letter that was to carry such pain to her son across the sea.

When the bitter task was over she threw herself upon a low divan and wept bitterly a long, long while, almost frightened at what she had done.

She feared that she could not mold her son's will to compliance by harshness as easily as she had done that of his timid sister.

"But he will not give up everything—he could not be so rash—for the sake of a fair-faced girl," she told herself, with faint flickering hope.

Several hours later Alva entered the room, still in her rich carriage-dress, her face pale and grave.

"Oh, mamma, I have had a great shock," she sighed.

"You did not find Cupid?"

"No, she had not come to the store this morning, but they told me where she boarded, and I drove there. Oh, what a terrible story I heard!"

"The girl had eloped, perhaps," smiled the lady.

"Worse than that. I've often regretted that I didn't elope myself when I was a girl," returned Alva, flippantly, then instantly grew serious again as she continued, sadly: "The poor girl, by some strange accident, fell from her window in the fourth story down to the street last evening, and was removed to Bellevue, unconscious, and believed to be dying."

"Oh, how sad, how shocking! and she was *so sweet!*" mused Mrs. Beresford, tenderly.

"So I drove to Bellevue, though expecting to find her dead," went on Alva. "And now, mamma, comes the strangest part of the story—my Cupid had been mysteriously spirited away from the hospital."

21

"ALVA!" CRIED MRS. Beresford, gazing at her daughter in consternation.

She grew pale and shuddered as she spoke, for the thought of the lovely girl's terrible accident touched her deeply.

"Is it not a terrible disappointment?" cried Alva. "Perhaps I shall never find her now, and my 'Cupid' will never be finished."

"But surely the girl will be found again!" Mrs. Beresford cried, consolingly, but Alva shook her head.

"I fear not, for her disappearance was so strange. Listen, mamma: they took her to Bellevue, and she did not recover consciousness the whole way. They supposed she would certainly die of her terrible fall. When they arrived at the hospital, she was left alone on a couch in the receiving-room for a few minutes, so the attendants say, and when the physician in charge went to see about her case, the little beauty was gone—had vanished as entirely as if she had been snatched up into the sky or swallowed by the earth, and left not a trace behind."

Mrs. Beresford smiled, and said:

"But, as we know that neither one of those things happened to her, we may hope that she is safe. My own theory is that she was unhurt by the fall, and simply fainted from the shock. When she recovered from her swoon, she doubtless became alarmed at finding herself alone in that strange place, and ran away in a fright."

"Yes, that is what they think at the hospital, but what became of her, mamma, *afterward*?"

She paused a moment, then added, anxiously:

"You see, that was the day before yesterday, and she never returned to her boarding-house nor the store. So—*where is she now?*"

And that question, asked by Mrs. Beresford's pale lips, became the text on which many changes were rung afterward.

A beautiful young girl had disappeared in the strangest way, and no clue to the mystery could be found.

The hospital authorities, fearing they might be accused of neglect in the matter, kept the occurrence as quiet as possible, and when some rumor of it reached the ubiquitous reporter, and he came to make inquiries, they told him the girl was all right—oh, yes, and had returned to her friends in New Jersey. She had written back to say that she had recovered from her swoon and ran away in a fright, that was all. Might he see the letter? Certainly.

But a hasty search proved unavailing. They were sorry, very sorry, but it must have gone into the wastebasket.

So the reporter, satisfied that there was no sensation in the case, withdrew, and sought a spicy paragraph for his paper elsewhere. But all the same, he had been cleverly gulled and cheated out of an interesting item.

For the mystery of Florence Fane's disappearance became one of the most unfathomable on record.

The fair young girl returned neither to her New York boarding-house, nor to the store where she was employed, nor to her Mount Vernon home.

It was not until a week had passed, and poor Mrs. Banks was beginning to fret over the non-reception of letters from Floy, that she was told the terrible truth of the girl's disappearance.

But, prompted by Otho, they made light of the matter, declaring that the giddy young girl would turn up when least expected. No doubt she had gone to stay with some new friends she had made in New York.

Poor Mrs. Banks was heart-broken, but she could do nothing. Poverty tied her hands from making any search for her darling. She could only pine and endure in silence.

The Maurys did not see that there was anything to do but wait for developments.

In all the world there seemed to be no friend to seek for the missing girl.

And yet, undreamed of by the Maurys, there was a search going on for Floy.

It seemed like a grim mocking of fate that the Beresfords, who would have rejoiced to hear of the death of George's sweetheart, should have put themselves to great expense to trace Florence Fane in her mysterious disappearance. Yet they had done so.

Mrs. Beresford was at heart a noble lady, and, where personal pride did not goad her to extremes, a firm friend.

She had taken a strong, admiring interest in the pretty young salesgirl whose beauty had charmed her, and whose pride had amused her while it also inspired respect.

She would not have owned it to herself, but Floy's blue eyes had looked straight into her heart and won herself a place there.

She had conceived the idea of employing the young girl to act as a model for Alva, and her disappointment was almost as keen as Alva's when she learned the truth.

Each day they both felt the disappointment more keenly, until from the mother came the startling suggestion:

"Why not put a private detective on her track?"

"Mamma, you seem to feel sure that the girl is alive, while on my side I think that her brain was injured by her terrible fall, and that she left the hospital in a dazed condition and met death in her wanderings."

"I have a strange feeling that the girl is alive and will be found again, dear, so I shall put a detective on the case at once," returned Mrs. Beresford, and she sent for one in whom she knew she could place confidence, and sent him on the quest.

22

THE CLEVER DETECTIVE was not the only person who was furtively engaged in an eager search for the missing girl.

Otho Maury, although he had written falsely to George Beresford that Floy was dead, had learned already, to his dismay, of her strange disappearance.

He saw that matters were more complicated than ever.

Floy was alive, he felt sure, and he foreboded that she would be turning up at some inopportune moment in Maybelle's path, and blocking her way to success with Beresford.

He guessed readily enough that Floy had become frightened at his persecutions, and had hidden herself away from him, awaiting Beresford's return.

And at the bare thought of Beresford's possessing the enchanting little beauty, Otho's jealous blood leaped like fire along his veins, and he swore to himself that he would rather murder Floy with his own hands than to witness her happiness with his splendid, noble rival.

Again he held a secret conference with his sister, and she raged with anger when she learned of Floy's escape from death.

"You have botched everything, and I shall lose the man I love, after all!" she cried, stormily, and her brother, unmoved by her blame, replied, coldly:

"Your chances certainly do not appear good at present, but I will continue to do the best I can for your interests. But the game is in fate's hands, and will be hard won, if won at all."

"If you could only find her and put her out of the way," she muttered, darkly.

"I will try," he answered, and it was tacitly understood between them that the contest against Floy's life and honor was to be waged more persistently than ever.

Let her but be found again, and Otho swore that he would make it impossible for her to marry Beresford.

Oh, it was cruel, shameful, wicked, this terrible warfare against a helpless orphan girl to whom life might otherwise have proved so bright and fair!

It was a wonder that peaceful sleep could visit the pillows of the two arch-plotters, Otho and Maybelle.

Yet the girl dreamed of a future wherein Floy should be swept from her path and Beresford won at last, while Otho—well, as for Otho, the future did not look so bright.

He loved Floy, and the plot against her, though he never swerved from it, planted thorns in his own heart.

So he took up the quest for the hapless little beauty, and when all inquiry failed in New York and Mount Vernon, he was obliged to consider himself baffled.

"I wish I had the powers of an amateur detective," he thought, longingly, but he did not dare to employ one.

And he would have been startled if he had known that he was under the espionage of the best private detective in New York.

For Mrs. Beresford's clever employee in pursuing his search for Floy, had informed himself first of all as to whether the young girl had a lover.

He found out that Otho Maury had paid her marked attention, and while he pursued his search for Floy he kept a careful eye on her lover.

And his first suspicion that Otho might know the girl's whereabouts was soon dissipated by finding out that Otho was as keenly on the alert as himself.

So the mystery deepened.

Neither lover nor detective could find one trace of bonny Floy after her flight from Bellevue that fateful twenty-first of May.

The detective went down to Mount Vernon and spent a week. He found out everything about the girl, save and except that George Beresford had been her accepted over. That affair had been so brief that none guessed it save Otho and Maybelle.

Floyd Landon, the detective, intercepted Mrs. Banks in one of her visits to the cemetery, and in a casual way, introduced himself, hoping to find out something more. She was quite willing to talk on the beloved subject, but she could tell no more than the neighbors had told already—the story of Suicide Place, and the pretty child the kind carpenter had taken from her dead mother's arms and brought to their humble cottage to be their own thereafter.

"And," sobbed the broken-hearted widow, looking down with streaming eyes at the lonely grave, "we loved her just as dearly as if she had been our own flesh and blood, and if my poor John knew what she has come to now, I don't believe he could rest in his grave."

"It was very noble in you both to care for her as you did," said Floyd Landon, and a minute later he asked, thoughtfully: "In case of her being proved dead, who will inherit Suicide Place?"

"I don't know, sir—there are no relatives alive that I'm aware of. It seemed like Floy was the last of her line."

"And you do not believe that she has followed the example of her race and cut herself off from life?"

Mrs. Banks shuddered.

"Oh, no, sir, I cannot believe that she would do that. She always laughed at the notion, and never showed any superstition but once."

His persuasive gaze coaxed her to proceed with her confidences.

"It was the night before she went away to be a salesgirl in the great city," continued Mrs. Banks. "We sat up late talking, and sweet little Floy said, humbly:

"'There's one thing I must confess to you, auntie: I've often disobeyed your orders and gone into Suicide Place alone. Will you forgive me now?'

"'Oh my dear, how could you venture near that terrible place?' I cried, in alarm. Then, seeing the paleness of her sweet face, I added: 'I forgive you, dear, but you must never venture near that place again.'

"'No, I *never* shall!' cried Floy, with the greatest energy. Clasping her pretty little hands together, she went on, tremblingly: 'I went there once too often, auntie, dear, and I found out the— the—I found out that the old place is haunted, as people say, and I think I understand the malign influence there that drives people to madness and suicide.'

"I begged her to tell me all, but she refused, growing pale, and trembling like a leaf in a storm, as she added:

"'I must not tell anyone. It is an accursed knowledge, and brings doom on those who learn it—a terrible doom! Oh, I used to laugh at the croakers, but now I know they were right. I have seen the horror that haunts the place. I know the secret hidden in those old stone walls. But it shall not destroy me, auntie, dear, for I will shun it like the plague. Never will I cross that fatal threshold again, and if I am ever rich enough, I shall have the house torn down stone by stone, and let in the light of day on the earth it covers, so that there shall be no more curse upon it!'"

"And she would tell you no more, madame?"

"Not one word more, and the next day she went away from me, my pretty darling, to be lost in the mysteries of that wicked New York!" sobbed the poor woman.

"Do you really believe that Suicide Place is haunted, Madame?"

"Oh, yes, sir, certainly. Everyone says so, and lights have been seen in the windows many a dark night, though the place hasn't had a tenant these nine years and more. 'Tis said that evil spirits haunt the place and drive the tenants to madness or suicide."

Her story was interesting, but it threw no light on the deep mystery of Florence Fane's fate.

So he went back to New York to tell his wealthy patron that he had failed in his quest.

"I have learned all that was possible to find out about her," he said. "It is agreed by all who know her that she was lovely and fascinating to a high degree. She had many admirers, but she had laughed at them in her pretty, saucy fashion, and all believed that she was heart-whole and fancy-free."

He found Mrs. Beresford and Alva so strangely interested in the young girl's fate that he told them all he had heard at Mount Vernon of her romantic story, and added:

"It seems likely that there is a stain of madness in the blood leading ultimately to suicide. This young girl, inheriting this terrible taint, and suffering an aberration of mind from her fall, may have fled from the hospital straight to the cold embrace of the river."

They shuddered, the two beautiful, high-born women, at his words, but Mrs. Beresford said quickly:

"Although it is a plausible theory, there is one weak point in it."

Landon looked at her inquiringly, and she said:

"If a strain of madness in the race led its members to suicide, why did one who was alien to them—a hired man on the place, I think you said—prove the victim in one decade?"

"That fact escaped my mind while I was speaking," he replied, "so my theory really has no ground to stand on. The horror-haunted house must really have some malign influence, must be haunted, as the young girl averred."

"It is a strange story you have told us, Mr. Landon, and makes the young girl more interesting to us than before. I hope you will not entirely give up the search, for success would be liberally rewarded," said Mrs. Beresford, as she handed him a munificent check for his two weeks' services.

He bowed himself out, and then the mask of conventionality fell from the proud woman's face, and it grew sad to the verge of tears.

"Oh, my son, my son!" she sobbed under her breath, and the thought of him was like a sword in her wounded heart.

She had that day received from George the sorrowful letter in which he had renounced home and wealth for Love's sake.

Bitter was her anger, deep the wound in her heart, as she read the brief, manly words.

"He is stubborn, foolish!" she cried, as she flung the letter to Alva.

Her queenly daughter read it, and smiled her light, cynical smile.

"How brave he is, how loyal to his love! I see now that he was in earnest, and I admire him more than ever!" she exclaimed.

"Alva!" reproachfully.

"I mean it all, mamma! I—I would not have my brother's heart tortured as mine was in my spring of youth."

"Have we not humored every other whim, my darling?"

"You have been most indulgent, but—" and Alva broke off with a long, quivering sigh. She was thinking:

Thou canst not restore me the depth and the truth
Of the dreams that came o'er me in earliest youth;
Their gloss is departed, their magic is flown,
And sad and faint-hearted I wander alone.

"His father will be bitterly angry," said Mrs. Beresford, sighing.

"Very likely," Alva returned, indifferently.

"I am sorry you take sides with your brother against us," stiffly.

Alva laughed drearily, then said, coldly:

"I glory in his independence!"

23

OTHO MAURY RECEIVED no answer to the letter he so art-
fully sent to George Beresford.

But he had not expected a reply. He knew that the blow must
fall with too crushing a weight on the lover's heart to admit of
comment, and he knew also that Beresford would never forgive
him for his offense against Floy.

He gave up the quest for the missing girl after two weeks, and
went back to Mount Vernon distracted with doubt and fear.

"I am all at sea," he confessed, frankly, to Maybelle, who grew
pale with anger as she cried:

"You have failed!"

"Yes, I have failed. There is no clue to her disappearance. She
may possibly be dead, but the probabilities are that, frightened by
my persecution, she has hidden herself away from all who know
her to baffle persecution until Beresford's return. Let us hope that
she is dead."

"She is not dead. She will live to thwart all our hopes!" cried
his sister, furiously.

Springing to her feet, she stood before him, livid with emotion, hissing:

"Oh, how I hate that girl! I wish that I had killed her last night
when I had her in my power!"

"Last night, Maybelle! Why, what do you mean?" he exclaimed
in wonder, clutching her arm and forcing her back to a seat.

Maybelle leaned back panting and unnerved for a moment,
then cried, bitterly:

"I was a fool to be frightened and take her for a ghost!"

"Calm yourself, Maybelle, and tell me what you mean," Otho
insisted, excitedly.

Fixing her flashing eyes on his face, she said, hoarsely:

"Do you know that all the talk for several days has been that Floy's ghost has been seen several times in Mount Vernon in the past two weeks?"

"No—no."

"Well, it is true, Otho. She has been seen three times, they say, by townspeople, twice on foot, and one night on her bicycle. But when spoken to, she did not reply, and vanished like a spirit. So they say that she is surely dead."

He started, and his eyes flashed as he cried:

"But you, Maybelle? —you said you saw her last night! Where?"

"Here, Otho, in this very house!"

"Heavens! then she must be in collusion with Mrs. Banks."

"No, she is not. The woman firmly believes that her *protégée* is dead."

"Then tell me all. Do you not see how impatient you have made me with your mysterious hints?"

She leaned nearer to him and whispered, hoarsely:

"She was here in this house at midnight last night. I was lying asleep on my bed. The windows were raised, for the air was oppressively warm. Then, too, I liked to smell the mingled odors of rose and honeysuckle clambering up the trellis. It was clear, bright moonlight, so I extinguished my lamp when I retired."

"Yes, yes, go on, Maybelle!" breathed Otho, impatiently.

"I fell asleep, and rested calmly until about midnight, when I awakened in a fright, for someone was shaking me rudely.

"'Get up—get up, Maybelle Maury! I want the letters my lover wrote me—the letters you have stolen!' cried an angry voice.

"I started bolt upright in bed, frightened almost to death, and half-dazed by being so suddenly roused from sleep, and there before me was that little vixen Floy, all in ghastly white, her golden hair all in a fluff over her head like a halo. She stood in a patch of white moonlight that made her look ethereal, and in my confusion I really took her for a ghost!"

"Pshaw!" exclaimed Otho, impatiently, and Maybelle said, deprecatingly:

"You must remember that I was roused from sleep and taken by surprise, or I should not have been so easily deceived. And she was so imperative, she did not give me time to collect my thoughts, but went on, angrily:

"'Get up, Maybelle Maury, you wicked, wicked girl, and give me my letters this minute, or I will go to your Mother and tell her how cruelly you and Otho have treated me! You will not enjoy that, for your mother is a good woman. She would be shocked if she knew that you told the postman a lie that you might get my letters and keep them from me.'"

"She did not talk much like a ghost," interpolated Otho.

"No, she did not, but I was so dazed and frightened I did not realize it then. And the little vixen kept scolding and threatening and pointing her finger at me until I felt like one under a hypnotic spell, and afraid to disobey, so, following the pointing of her finger, I rose from my bed, staggered tremblingly to my desk, and handed her the package of letters I had intercepted. Then, overcome by horror, I fell unconscious upon the bed. When I revived, my midnight visitor had disappeared."

"It was Floy herself!" declared Otho, with bitter chagrin.

"Yes, I am certain of it—have not doubted it since I came to my sober senses," answered Maybelle, with a choking sigh of futile rage. "Oh, how I hate myself," she continued, "for giving her those letters! She is gloating over them—rejoicing at every tender word—while I—I could strangle her with my own hands for her triumph over me!"

"And I!" cried Otho, burning with murderous jealousy at thought of Floy's innocent joy at the recovery of her love letters.

He could fancy what tender words Beresford would write to his darling, and how her eyes would beam with joy as she read them over.

He felt, like Maybelle, that he would like to strangle the joy in her sweet white throat with murderous hands.

24

"I AM SORRY now that I did not follow my first impulse and burn those hateful letters!" cried Maybelle regretfully.

"How many were there?" asked her brother, grimly.

"Seven in all. He must have written to her every day until he received your letter that she was dead. And such letters! fully of the silliest love. Pah!" cried the girl, who despised the letters because they were written to her rival.

If they had been intended for her—jealous, envious Maybelle—she would have wished them framed in gold and precious stones.

For what is so dear to a woman's heart as a love letter from the man she adores?

The mere sight of it makes the blood bound gladly through her frame, and brightens eye and cheek with joy.

The touch of it makes her fingers tingle with delight.

She reads it over and over in the solitude of her own chamber, and kisses it as fondly as if it were the face of her beloved.

She carries it in her bosom by day, and places it beneath her pillow, to bring blissful dreams, by night.

All this bliss of which Maybelle had robbed bonny Floy was hers now, and the angry girl's bosom throbbed with the awful pain of jealousy as she realized how her sweet rival would rejoice over those ardent words of love sprinkled like diamonds over the pages he had written for her comfort while they were sundered one from each other:

I thought of thee—I thought of thee
On ocean many a weary night,
When heaved the long and solemn sea,
With only waves and stars in sight.
We stole along by aisles of balm,

We furled before the coming gale,
We slept amid the breathless calm,
We flew before the straining sail—
But thou wert lost alas! to me,
And day and night I thought of thee.

Otho listened to his sister with a cynical frown, guessing all that she suffered by the pain in his own heart.

"I have a suspicion!" he exclaimed, abruptly.

"What is it?"

"Floy is hidden at Suicide Place," he said, with an evil gleam in his deep-set, dark eyes.

"Do you think so? But Floy told Mrs. Banks before she went away that she had seen something terrible there, and would never cross the threshold again."

"No matter. I believe she is in hiding there. It is so simple a solution of the mystery that I wonder it did not occur to me before. Yes, she is surely at Suicide Place, and I shall entrap her tonight!" he exclaimed, with triumphant malice.

"But Otho, are you not afraid to venture into that fatal house?"

"Not in the least. I prize my life too highly ever to commit suicide, I assure you. I am strong-minded, practical. The grim influence of the place will not affect me."

"I am glad that you think so, and I hope that you prosper in your undertaking tonight."

"Thank you, sis, I cannot foresee any possible failure this time. She will be entirely at my mercy, with no Beresford to interfere."

They were both silent for a time, ashamed to discuss their wicked plans, then Maybelle drew a deep breath, exclaiming:

"Whatever is done it must be ended soon, for it is three weeks now since he sailed, and he expected to return in a month."

"Her fate will be sealed before then," Otho answered, quickly, and added: "If you are ever to win Beresford, it must be done quickly also, for father is on the verge of failure, though reputed a millionaire."

"On the verge of failure—oh, heavens! That is why he refused me the new set of diamonds I craved! Oh, Heaven help me to win Beresford, for I could not endure a life of poverty!" exclaimed Maybelle, hysterically.

"I do not see how I am to endure it either, but I did not seem to make any progress with the heiress," grumbled Otho.

"You did not, for she showed her indifference too plainly to encourage the least hope," agreed his sister, frankly.

"Curse her for a proud, haughty jade, but I do not care for her any way. My heart is set on bewitching little Fly-away Floy."

"Then why not marry her, Otho, if you care so much, since that would take her from Beresford as effectually as if she were dead?"

"She would not marry me to save my life, the proud little minx! But I'll have my revenge for her scorn, never fear, and leave the field clear for you to win Beresford," laughed Otho, gratingly.

"Oh, if you succeed, I shall pay you well out of my husband's riches," she cried, eagerly.

"You may not get the handling of many dollars, and my demands will be exorbitant," he grumbled, sighing: "I wish that the foul fiend would deign to show me some royal road to fortune."

It was an aspiration he had uttered often before in his greed for gold and his impatience of his father's restraints, and no thought came to him that it would be granted soon.

Rejoicing in his good luck at finding Floy's hiding-place at last, he waited most impatiently for the close of the beautiful June day that he might sally forth on his dastardly errand.

The sun set in a blaze of golden glory, and the young moon rose over the tree-tops, shedding a tender amber light upon the quiet, resting world.

As soon as he could get away unobserved, Otho took the lonely road toward Suicide Place.

"She cannot escape me now, my pretty Floy!" he muttered.

25

"OH, MY DARLING, a whole lifetime of devotion shall teach you the strength of my love. Your life with me, my bonny bride, shall be a dream of bliss."

Floy's big, starry-blue eyes glowed like blue jewels in the dusk as she read aloud the tender words of her lover's letter.

Then she pressed her rosy lips to the page as fondly as though it had been the handsome face of her absent love.

"How he loves me, my noble, splendid, beautiful, dark-eyed lover! He has chosen me, simple little Floy, poor and obscure, out of a whole world of rich and beautiful girls, any one of whom must have loved him if he had so chosen," she cried in an ecstasy of adoring love.

She was alone in a large, gloomy bedroom of Suicide Place, for, as Otho had suspected, on hearing Maybelle's story today, she was here in hiding from her foes.

She had been most indiscreet in her adventure last night, but the longing to possess the letters Beresford had written to her overpowered every other impulse, so, trusting that Maybelle might take *her* for a ghost, the brave little beauty made a determined onslaught and secured her own property, escaping undetected through the open window that looked upon an upper veranda wreathed in fragrant vines.

"What a wretch she was to obtain my letters in that fashion! I am glad I thought of going to see the good carrier and finding out the truth, or I never should have had these sweet words to read!" cried Floy, kissing them again, as she had done dozens of times already today.

In the falling twilight she sat at the upper window behind the lace curtain that screened her from view outside, and read and reread the precious trophies in artless delight, her heart throbbing fast with joy at each tender word.

"What a fortunate girl I am to have won such a splendid lover!" she thought, with innocent pride and exultation, for her tender young heart yearned for love and care, she was so lonely.

Floy did not realize all her great charms of mind and person, and in her lack of vanity she was always wondering how the splendid Beresford had chosen her so quickly for his heart's queen out of a whole world full of lovely girls.

> *I seek you—you alone I seek;*
> *All other women fair*
> *Or wise or good may go their way,*
> *Without my thought or care.*
> *But you I follow day by day,*
> *And night by night I keep*
> *My heart's chaste mansion lighted, where*
> *Your image lies asleep.*
> *Asleep! If e'er to wake, He knows*
> *Who Eve to Adam brought,*
> *As you to me, the embodiment*
> *Of boyhood's dear, sweet thought.*
> *And youth's fond dream, and manhood's hope,*
> *That still half hopeless shone,*
> *Till every rootless, vain ideal*
> *Commingled into one—*
> *You, who are so diverse from me,*
> *And yet as much my own*
> *As this my soul, which formed a part,*
> *Dwells in its bodily throne.*
> *I swear no oaths, I tell no lies,*
> *Nor boast I never knew*
> *A love dream—we all dream in youth—*
> *But, waking, I found you—*
> *The real woman, whose first touch*
> *Aroused to highest life*
> *My real manhood. Crown it, then,*
> *Good angel, friend, love, wife!*

"Oh, what lovely words and thoughts!" cried Floy, reading them again for the twentieth time, and she added, half in pity for cruel, jealous Maybelle: "How it must have stabbed her heart to

read these tender words addressed to me! It must have been punishment enough for all her sin."

She was right, for what could be more cruel pain to a jealous,
envious heart than to read those words of love to another?

> *He loves, but 'tis not me he loves,*
> *Not me on whom he ponders,*
> *When in some dream of tenderness*
> *His truant fancy wanders.*

The purple gloaming deepened, the shadows grew darker in
the gloomy room, until even the eyes of love could not distinguish
the written words, so Floy laid her letters upon the little table before her, and fell to dreaming over them in tender wise:

"*Seven* letters! and such beautiful *long* ones, too! Oh, how good
he was to write me such charming love letters! Can such love ever
grow cold, I wonder? Can he ever look back and regret? Ah, no,
no, no! I will not remember the stories of false love I have read
and heard. He, my own dark-eyed lover, is not one of those fickle
wretches flying from one love to another, like a butterfly from
flower to flower. He will be true."

A happy sigh escaped her lips, and she continued:

"It is terrible being shut up here like a prisoner, with nothing
to eat but half-ripe fruit picked from the orchard by night! I wish
I dared reveal myself to Auntie Banks and beg her to come here
and share my solitude. But she wouldn't consent, I know, and
those wretches would contrive some new peril for me, if they
found out I was alive. Oh, dear Heaven, give me patience to bear
this life till my lover returns! It is only a few days more now, for
he said he should not stay longer than a month. He will think it
strange I did not answer his letters, as he told me to do in each
loving postscript, but I can easily explain all to him when I see
him, and he will not blame me for not writing when he knows I
did not get his letters for so long."

Poor Floy, counting the days and hours before her over's return, how little she dreamed that far across the sea he lay ill unto
death, stricken down by the false and cruel story that she was
dead.

The hours waned, and the moon rose in the purple sky, while she lingered there, poor child, so lonely in her exile, so beautiful, so unfortunate.

She rose presently, drew the shutters close, then lighted a little lamp on the table, not caring much if the light was seen by passers-by, for she knew no one would venture in. She had heard stories often of lights being seen in the house by night, but they were all attributed to ghostly visitants.

Floy knew the ghastly secret of Suicide Place now, and nothing but her terror of Otho Maury would have tempted her to enter the house again.

But when she had recovered consciousness at Bellevue Hospital the evening of her accident, and found herself uninjured, an awful fear of Otho Maury's persecutions entered her mind.

"Oh, if I could hide myself away from him somewhere until George's return," she moaned.

She had a subtle presentiment that Otho's persecutions would ruin her life if his nefarious plans were not balked.

"Oh, I must hide myself from that black-hearted wretch!" she sobbed, sitting up on the couch, and gazing wildly around.

She saw that she was quite alone, the attendant having gone to hasten the physician whose duty it was to attend to her case.

The thought of Suicide Place came to her like an inspiration, and she sighed to herself that all its horrors were not equal to Otho Maury's relentless pursuit.

She staggered to her feet and found herself unhurt. The long swoon had been the result of the shock of fear.

Pursued by fear and unrest, Floy fled wildly from the hospital, and as she had on her person the five dollars given her by Mrs. Banks, she made use of it to return to Mount Vernon.

That night she rested in the haunted house, that, with its evil repute, seemed to offer her a refuge from despair.

Here, during the two weeks while the search for her went on, Floy rested safe from pursuit.

But her adventurous spirit drove her forth at last to inquire of the letter-carrier about the mail she had expected to receive from Beresford. Without acquainting him with her hiding-place, she pledged him to secrecy over her visit, and obtained from him the information that Miss Maury had intercepted her letters.

She made several futile trips to the Maury residence before she succeeded in getting possession of the precious letters.

Having purposely made herself look as phantom-like as possible, she was seen by several persons, and the report that her spirit walked became noised about.

Having obtained the letters, she resolved not to venture forth again, lest she should be followed and her identity discovered.

But, as we have seen, by Maybelle's story, her discretion came too late, and she was fated to a severe ordeal—the result of last night's adventure.

Through the fragrant gloom of the summer night Otho Maury was gliding toward the house, wriggling his lean body through the shadows like a hungry panther about to spring upon its prey, and as his stealthy step pressed the threshold, he kept muttering, darkly, with horrible exultation:

"She cannot escape me now!"

26

THE ROOM WHERE Floy sat had been her mother's bedchamber. It was a large, handsome apartment, with stenciled walls and deep mahogany wainscoting after the old style, and the dark, massive furniture was of the richest mahogany. The dark polished floor was covered with rich rugs from Persia, and a magnificent full-length mirror between the two windows had reflected many a beautiful face and form of Floy's ancestors.

They had been handsome people, the Nellests, but Floy's beauty was of quite a different type.

Her mother had been dark and stately, like all the Nellests, but Floy was fair as Venus fresh risen from the foam. She had inherited her blonde beauty from her English father, as also her sunny, happy nature. The Nellests had been cold, grave, severe people, given to moroseness on account of their loss of fortune sixty years ago.

They had been rich and grand in their day, and the first suicide in the family dated from the time when the death of the head of the house revealed the appalling fact that the family was beggared, nothing remaining of vast wealth but the fine farm—their summer residence.

It was incredible, for old Jasper Nellest had been miserly in his way, and it was supposed that under his management the property must have increased instead of dwindling.

His two sons, both married and fathers of families, investigated matters, and found that their father had turned everything he possessed—bonds, houses, land, and ships upon the sea—into hard, yellow, shining gold.

What had become of this great treasure?

They found out that he had also been a heavy and reckless stock gambler, and this seemed to account for everything.

The mad thirst for speculation had swallowed up everything. Having staked all and lost, he died without confessing that he had beggared his family.

But, as his death had been a swift and sudden one, from apoplexy, there had been no time for death-bed disclosures.

But neither did Jasper Nellest leave any papers bearing on the subject of his lost wealth.

He had simply possessed it, and made "ducks and drakes" of it. That was the situation that stared his descendants in the face.

The brothers began an unequal struggle with the world as poor men with dependent families.

The elder one suicided within a decade, and the younger dragged the weary chain of life until he was sixty, then death released him.

But along the path of their descendants each decade was marked by a suicide in the morose family, and they decreased in numbers until the unfortunate line had almost died out. Only Floy was left now—fairest and most unfortunate of her race.

The shadows of fate had indeed fallen most heavily on that little golden head.

Bereaved of all who loved her, bound in the cruel toils of poverty, sundered from her lover, in hiding from relentless foes—alas, poor little Floy!

In sorrow did your life begin,
Dark lines of fate have hedged it in;
Yet is your face as bright and fair
As if the shadow of black care
Threw over it no dismal gloom—
A cloud between you and earth's bloom.
"The blue of heaven is in your eyes,
The heavens' o'erarching paradise;
The sunshine's gold doth crown your head
Your pouting lips are cherry-red;
The lily's whiteness doth bedeck
The soft curves of your dimpled neck,
And on your cheek in beauty glows
And faint blush of the opening rose.

Floy paced up and down the room awhile, yawned and threw herself down again in a chair at the window.

"How slowly the time goes!" she sighed. "I wish I *did* have a lock to that door! But I don't suppose anything human will annoy me here. Otho Maury *would*, I know, if he dreamed that I was here, but, of course, he is searching for me in New York, hoping all the while that I'm dead and out of Maybelle's way. Oh-h-h! what was *that*?"

She shuddered and groaned, for a sound had reached her ears in the awfully still old house—an eerie sound!

It came up from the parlor below, and sounded like a discord played by unskilled hands upon the piano keys.

It had been caused, in fact, by Otho Maury, stumbling against the piano, in his furtive search for Floy.

Floy's heart thumped terrifically against her side for a moment, then she recovered herself as memory recalled her first night at Suicide Place.

"It's just the mice running over the piano keys," she laughed.

A full half an hour passed, and she grew nervous and restless, startled by muffled sounds of footsteps in the house.

"What can it be? —the wind or the rats?" she muttered, in alarm. "I have never heard such strange noises in the house before. Can anyone have dared enter?"

Instinctively she caught up a dagger that she had found in a drawer of the old-fashioned bureau and laid on the table for self-protection.

Drawing the keen, shining blade from its sheath, she held it in her hand, her flashing eyes turned toward the door.

"Let any intruder dare enter here, and I will sell my life and honor dearly!" she cried.

27

AS IF IN answer to her defiance, a stealthy hand turned the knob, the door swung lightly back, and the form of a man stood hesitating on the threshold.

"Otho Maury!"

The cry shrilled over her lips in a strangled gasp of loathing—not fear, for with that weapon in her hand she felt strong to defy the villain.

He started, and stood looking at her with dazed eyes.

He had searched the whole house over by the aid of a dark lantern, and almost began to despair of success, when he opened this last door.

He found her there, beautiful, brave, defiant, her angry blue eyes fixed on him, and her white hand grasping the weapon whose shining blade would surely be sheathed in his heart if he dared approach the little beauty.

After his first start of surprise he cried, longingly:

"Floy!"

She saw that he was deathly pale, and heard a strange tremor in his voice.

"He is frightened, and I shall easily drive him off," she thought, exultantly, and replied:

"How dare you intrude yourself into this house again, Otho Maury? Have you forgotten how you were punished the last time?"

He glared angrily at her, and returned:

"No, but Beresford is not here to save you now."

"But I can defend myself!" she cried, defiantly, brandishing her weapon.

"Put down that child's toy, my dear. I am not afraid of it in the least. I could take it from you and snap it like a twig!"

"You *are* afraid, you wretch! Your face is ashen pale and your voice trembles with fear!" she retorted, confidently.

"If my face is pale, and my voice weak, it is not from fear of that shining little blade in your tiny hand, it is from horror at what I have seen since I entered this house. Tell me, Floy, did you know that this house is really haunted?"

"Yes, I knew it," she answered, and her voice grew tremulous also, while a look of horror dawned in her eyes.

"You knew it!" he cried in wonder. "Then how have you had the courage to remain here alone?"

"You do well to ask that question," the poor girl cried out, bitterly. "You, Otho Maury, who have almost hounded me to death. Stay! do not advance one step nearer, or—"

He drew back sullenly, and remained on the threshold facing her with his back to the dark corridor, while he said, pleadingly:

"Floy, I followed you here with an honorable object. I love you madly. Will you become my wife?"

"Never!" she answered, curtly, with measureless contempt that angered him to frenzy.

"Take care how you scorn me, pretty Floy, for you are in my power, and I may take a terrible revenge for your contempt," he exclaimed, advancing toward her, secure in his ability to disarm the weak, puny girl.

"Heaven help me!" silently prayed the poor girl, bracing herself to drive home her weapon of defense into her assailant's breast as soon as he came within reach.

"If you come within reach, you are rushing on your death!" she cried, wildly.

"Ha! ha!" he laughed, as at some pretty child, and made a rush sidewise, aiming to wrench away the weapon, and, in spite of her alertness, he grasped the middle of the arm that held the dagger.

Like a flash, Floy transferred it to her other hand and struck out at random.

But the keen blade went home, piercing the side of his neck through, and as the blood spurted into his face, blinding him with its hot waves, he relaxed his hold and fell dizzily to the floor.

28

STILL GRASPING THE bloody weapon, Floy looked down in terror at the body of her bleeding victim.

"Oh-h-h! I have killed the mean coward, but—I couldn't help it—I had to do it!" she exclaimed, bursting into hysterical sobs.

"Bravo, miss, that was a brave deed! He deserved death, but if you had waited a minute longer, I would have killed him for you myself!" exclaimed an admiring voice, and a man who had been watching and listening in the corridor outside came hastily into the room.

He was a stranger to Floy, but you and I, reader, know him as the clever detective who had been searching for our heroine for several weeks.

Once he had decided that he would give up the hopeless quest, but his patron's anxiety spurred him on to another effort.

He returned to Mount Vernon, and when he heard the story of Floy's spirit having been seen abroad on several nights, he conceived a suspicion that the missing girl might be hidden at Suicide Place, in spite of her assertion that she would never venture near the house again.

Having no fear of ghosts, and laughing to himself at the idea of the place being haunted, he determined to search it for Floy.

He went upon the quest the same evening that Otho did, and arriving sometime later, went carefully round the house till he saw some gleams of light shining through the shutters.

"She is there!" he thought, exultantly, and went in through a door that Otho had carelessly left open.

Without taking the trouble to explore the lower regions, he made his way to the second story, following the location of the light he had detected.

When his stealthy steps reached the upper corridor he saw, to his amazement, a man stealing along in front of him, guided by a dark lantern.

The next moment he recognized him as Otho Maury, whose steps he had once dogged in the hope of discovering Floy.

"Aha! I was right after all. He *is* her lover. I will watch and see what comes of this!" he cried to himself, keeping at a safe distance behind Otho.

By this means he became an excited spectator of the tragic scene that followed, and learned how deeply Floy feared and dreaded her villainous persecutor.

He was springing into the room to her assistance, when the frantic thrust of her little dagger struck Maury at random in the neck, and stretched him bleeding at her feet.

At her sobs of terror and remorse—for it was awful to the gentle, white-souled girl to realize that she had taken life, even in self-defense—he cried, cheerily:

"Bravo, miss! that was a brave deed. He deserved death, but if you had waited a minute longer, I would have killed him for you myself."

Floy shrunk against the window, with a low cry of alarm, as she beheld this new intruder.

"Oh, God, why am I so bitterly persecuted?"

"I beg you not to be afraid of me, Floy. I am your friend," exclaimed the detective, kindly.

His voice sounded so honest and kindly that Floy said, faintly:

"Who are you? How came you here, sir?"

"I am Floyd Landon, a detective, miss, and I came here to search for you, but not with any evil intent, be sure, for I was employed by a true friend of yours, who will be delighted when I take you to her house."

Floy summoned courage to look at him, and saw that he was a good-looking, middle-aged person, with the frank, open face an honest countryman. No one would have suspected that he was one of the most successful detectives in the city of New York.

His heart was as kind as his face, too, and it was touched by the misery of the girl who was so remorseful over having destroyed a life.

Her beauty astonished him also, even though Mrs. Beresford's flattering description had prepared him in some measure for Floy's charms.

"A friend of mine!" she cried, in surprise. "Oh then it must have been Mrs. Banks. I think she is the only true friend I have in the world."

"No, it is not Mrs. Banks, it is another woman in the great city of New York."

"Not Mrs. Horton. She is no friend of mine!" cried Floy, who suspected the woman of having sent Otho Maury to her room that evening.

"Not Mrs. Horton," he replied, and bent down to look at Otho.

"His heart beats faintly. You have not killed him, miss— more's the pity, for he's only a human serpent," he added, under his breath.

"He's alive, you say? Oh, how glad I am! I did not want his death on my soul, though I hate and fear him!" cried Floy.

"Give me some water and a towel, miss, and I'll stanch the blood and see how bad the wound is," added the detective.

She brought the desired things, and as he went to work, he said:

"I was educated for a surgeon, so I know how to fix him all right. It's only a superficial wound through the side of his neck, and I can sew it up all right before he comes to himself."

He brought out a tiny surgical-case from his coat-pocket and sewed up the cut, after which he bandaged it nicely.

"Oh, how fortunate that you had those things along!" cried Floy, admiringly.

"Yes, they often come in handy in a detective's business as well as a surgeon's," smiled Floyd Landon. "So! he will do nicely, I think, and presently he will revive. Before then we must be out of the way."

29

FLOY LOOKED AT him inquiringly, and he said:

"Will you come with me tonight to New York and the lady who wants you so much, or shall you go to Mrs. Banks?"

"Not to her, though I love her dearly, for, oh! there is danger for me in her vicinity, since it is the home of Otho Maury, also. No, I must seek another hiding-place. Oh, sir, you look at me strangely! You do not understand my trouble, and I cannot explain it, for—for—I have a secret!" cried Floy, incoherently.

She looked down at Otho's face in alarm, crying:

"Oh, how ghastly he looks! Are you sure he is not really dead?"

"He is not dead, and will be able to devise new deviltry in a few weeks from now."

"Then let us hasten away. Who is the lady—the friend you said had employed you to find me?"

"Have you no suspicion?"

"Not the slightest," she replied, honestly.

"Did you ever meet a Mrs. Beresford in Maury's store in New York?"

Floy blushed divinely at the mention of the name of Beresford and exclaimed:

"Yes, I saw her once. She bought real lace handkerchiefs from me, and was so sweet and kind I have loved her memory ever since."

"She admired you very much," smiled the detective.

"She told me I was pretty—that she liked to look at me," confessed Floy, naïvely.

"Yes, that is it. She was charmed with your beauty, Floy, and I applaud her good taste," said Landon, admiringly, and continued: "Did you know that Mrs. Beresford's only daughter is a great artist?"

"I had not heard anything about her, sir."

"Well, it is true, and Mrs. Beresford saw that your face was the very one Miss Alva wanted as a model for a picture of Cupid that she is painting."

"Oh!" cried Floy, clasping her hands in wondering delight.

"So she told Miss Alva about you," continued the detective, "and they decided to try to secure you for a model, but when they went to the store—it was the day after the accident—you had disappeared. So they sent for me to find you."

He could not understand the wonderful radiance that came upon Floy's lovely face while he was speaking, making her beauty almost unearthly.

She was thinking, joyously:

"Oh, how blest I am that I have found favor with *his* mother—my darling's mother—and his gifted sister! They will take me into his dear home, and I will try to win their love, so that when he comes and finds me there they will be glad that I am his chosen one."

"Do you like the plan? Will you come with me to Mrs. Beresford?" asked Floyd Landon.

"Oh, so gladly—so gladly!" she cried, in a sort of rapture.

"Then let us lose no time in starting. And—hadn't you better find some sort of a disguise—a thick veil anyhow—so that you need not be recognized in going through the town?" he suggested.

Floy pulled open the drawers and found an old-fashioned traveling-wrap and thick veil and bonnet. She put these on in a hurry, and they left the house with its grim occupant, Otho Maury, lying silent on the floor, not yet revived from his long swoon.

No one would have recognized the detective's prim, old-fashioned-looking traveling companion as merry little Fly-away Floy. Her disguising costume was foreign in style, in fact, had been worn by her mother on her return from England.

30

"*I CAN NO* longer wonder at my mother's enthusiasm," thought Alva Beresford, on first beholding Floy.

It was not yet midnight when Floyd Landon arrived at the Fifth Avenue mansion with his charge.

He knew that it was late to intrude, but under the peculiar circumstances of the case, he deemed it best to waive ceremony and go at once to the house.

His arrival was timely, for Miss Beresford was just leaving her carriage on returning from a wedding-reception. She was in magnificent evening-dress, and the sheen of her diamonds fairly dazzled Floy's eyes as she gazed at the beautiful belle, while her features, so like those of her brother, made her fond heart leap wildly in her breast.

Floyd Landon presented his charge with a few explanatory words, and Miss Beresford was exceedingly gracious.

"So good of you to bring her to me at once," she cried, as she pressed Floy's little hand. "Now, you must come into the house and tell me all about it," she added, eagerly.

"I thank you, but the hour is late, and you must be weary after the evening's pleasure. I will postpone the telling until another time, if you will permit me," answered Floyd Landon, anxious to get home to his wife, whom he had left ailing when he went away that day.

"Tomorrow morning then, if you have leisure," replied the beautiful heiress, and after bidding him good night, she and Floy went up the white marble steps and into the house.

Floy felt like one in a blissful dream. In entering this splendid house, with its magnificent halls adorned with potted plants, glimmering statues, and costly paintings, she thought far less of the grandeur of the place than of the fact that it was the home of her lover.

Every association breathed of him, and made the strange house seem home-like at once to her fond, loving heart.

She felt herself blessed in the strange freak of Fate that had brought her to be a dweller beneath this roof.

"A few more days—just a few more days now—and he too, will be here, my love, my love!" throbbed her happy heart.

Alva led her upstairs to her own room, and summoned her maid.

"I have brought home a guest—Floy—who will serve me as a model in future. Arrange the blue room opposite mine for her occupancy," she said, in a tone that forbid curiosity.

When the maid had gone to do her bidding, she said, kindly:

"My dear, you look positively radiant somehow, yet surely you must be very tired."

"I am not tired—I have come only a short journey—from Mount Vernon—and I *am* so glad to be here, so glad that I can be of service to you, Miss Beresford, that every other emotion is swallowed up in pure joy!" exclaimed the grateful girl.

Alva looked admiringly at the lovely face with its radiant blue eyes and joy-flushed cheeks, and her heart went out to her strongly, tenderly.

"You are a sweet, lovely child!" she exclaimed, impulsively. "You have the most beautiful face in the world! It is no wonder my mother thought your face the ideal one for Cupid. Did you know that I wish to paint you as the little god of Love?"

"Is it so?" cried Floy, delightedly, and every moment she grew more lovely. The gladness of her heart was reflected charmingly in her face.

She had thrown off her disguising wraps, and in her simple attire was so lovely that Miss Beresford wondered how she would look in rich attire like her own—diamonds, laces, and rustling white satin.

"But she does not need them, she is lovely enough in her girl-ish bloom without adornment," she thought, quickly.

"I shall not ask you tonight to tell me where you have been hidden away so long, dear, for you must have your rest, but to-morrow, in my studio, you shall tell me everything," she said, as she conducted Floy to an exquisite room across the hall.

Floy looked about her in delight.

Was this beautiful room, all blue and silver, so dainty and bride-like, to be all her own, to sleep in and rest in day by day?

Alva saw her glance with secret perturbation at her cheap attire, and knew she was thinking of the contrast.

"You did not bring your trunk," she said, cheerfully. "Never mind, we will remedy all that tomorrow. I will send Honora shopping for you, and she has charming taste."

"You are too kind to me. I—I have no money, and—I cannot accept charity," faltered Floy, her sensitive pride taking alarm.

"You proud little Cupid, it will not be charity. Aren't you going to pose for me? I shall put your face into lovely pictures, and I shall have to pay you well for the privilege. The new outfit will be a payment in advance on my debt, that is all."

"Oh, thank you—thank you!" cried Floy, dimpling with delight at the thought of having new clothes when George came home.

"For I do not wish him to see me shabby and unsuited in my dress to my beautiful surroundings," she thought, with honest pride in herself.

Alva bid her a kind good-night and retired, leaving her in such a flutter of delight that it was several hours before her eyelids closed, thought and hope were so busy over the future.

The next morning she breakfasted alone with Alva and the latter said:

"I did not tell you last night that my parents sailed for Europe yesterday."

Floy looked so surprised that she added:

"They read in the paper a telegraphic dispatch from the London reporter that my brother George is quite ill in London."

"*Ill!*" almost shrieked poor Floy.

Her eyes drooped, her rosy face went white, she trembled so that Miss Beresford thought she was going to faint.

"My dear child, what is the matter—are you also ill?" she demanded, in alarm and surprise.

Floy recovered herself with an effort.

"Pardon me, I felt deathly sick for a moment," she faltered, then added: "I am afraid I lost what you were saying, Miss Beresford. But please go on. I am better now."

"I was saying that my brother is ill in London, and my parents sailed yesterday to bring him home as soon as he is better," replied Alva.

"Oh, I hope he is not very ill!" sighed Floy, very pale still, in spite of her declaration that she was better.

"Oh, no, I have no idea that there is much the matter with George, for he would have had his physician cable us, of course, if he had been really ill. These dispatches from foreign correspondents to their papers are often greatly exaggerated in the interests of sensationalism," replied Alva, carelessly, adding, after a moment: "But my parents fairly idolize their only son, so they took quick alarm and hurried over the sea to bring home the invalid."

They left the table, and Alva led Floy to her beautiful studio, where wealth and taste had united in adorning a most beautiful apartment. Priceless rugs covered part of the inlaid floor, and exquisite statues gleamed whitely from velvet-draped niches, while pictures were scattered everywhere, some framed, some in an unfinished condition on their easels, yet all showing the work of a master-hand. Here and there were vases of flowers perfuming the air with their sweetness, while silken curtains of rare design filtered the garish light of day into soft, rosy shadows.

Rich was the shadow of the room,
And bright the sifted sunlight's bloom,
That lofty wall and ceiling sheathed;
Heavy the perfumed air she breathed.
"Sumptuous sense of costly cheer
Pervaded the soft atmosphere,
As if charmed walls had shut it in
From all the wild world's noisy din.

Alva watched with delight Floy's keen appreciation of everything, as she wandered from picture to picture, drinking in their beauty with eager, appreciative eyes.

"She has a cultured soul, this lovely wildflower. I shall never be bored by her, no matter how much we are thrown together," thought Alva, gladly.

Then she drew the covering from her latest work and directed Floy to look at it.

The girl approached, and the first sight of the painting charmed her, it was so life-like—the dancing youths and maidens were so natural, the woods and water so perfect.

"Oh!" she cried, in an ecstasy, and Alva smiled, well pleased.

"You see it is not yet completed," she explained. "See there the figure of Cupid, with his bow and arrow. When I have given him your enchanting face, it will be finished, and I am so impatient to begin that I will commence painting this very morning!"

31

ALVA PAINTED UNWEARIEDLY for several hours, and declared herself charmed with her lovely, patient model.

Floy was enthusiastic, too. She declared that she could not be grateful enough to Miss Beresford for putting her face in that enchanting picture.

"Only think!" she cried. "When I am dead and gone—when the light has faded from my eyes—when this form of mine is dust in a forgotten grave—this beauty will live on upon the deathless canvas, and someone may say of me: 'She was so pretty, this little Floy Fane, that Miss Beresford made her face immortal by painting it as Cupid.'"

Alva saw that the girl's delight was genuine, and it charmed her very much.

"I shall put you in other pictures, too," she said. "Last night, after I left you, the thought came to me to paint your portrait in a simple white gown, and call it 'Maidenhood.' Do you like the idea?"

"I am charmed!" cried Floy.

"You remember Longfellow's 'Maidenhood'?" continued Alva, and she murmured some of the verses:

Maiden with the meek brown eyes,
In whose orbs a shadow lies,
Like the dusk in evening skies.
Thou whose locks outshine the sun,
Golden tresses wreathed in one,
As the braided streamlets run:
Standing with reluctant feet,
Where the brook and river meet,
Womanhood and childhood fleet.

"How old are you, Floy?"

"Almost seventeen."

"A charming age—the time of illusions! I am twenty-eight, dear—almost an old maid."

"You do not look twenty."

"So they tell me, but my heart is even older than my years," with a suppressed sigh, then, smiling: "Have you ever had a lover, Floy? Why, how frightened you look—how deeply you blush! Never mind. You needn't answer, child. Your face tells its own conscious story."

"Oh, if she only knew the name of that lover!" thought Floy, with quickened heartbeats, but she did not feel much frightened. She hoped that the haughty Beresfords who admired her so much would find it easy to forgive George for his choice.

But in the meantime she must keep her pretty secret, as he had commanded her to do. She would not tell them a word till he should take her by the hand and say:

"Pretty little Floy is my heart's choice."

How impatiently she waited for that day, only God and the angels knew.

For the thought of his illness and the secret terror that he might die, far away from his beloved, kept Floy awake many hours each night.

But if Alva were uneasy over her sick brother, she concealed it cleverly, or did not think that her pretty model had any interest in the subject, for she never mentioned it again until more than a week had passed away.

Then Floy, tortured by a secret unrest, cried out one day:

"Have you never heard from your parents yet?"

Alva was so busy she did not look around from her picture, and only answered:

"No. It is only a week since they went, you see, and they would not send a cablegram unless George was very ill. I dare say it was all a false alarm."

Floy feared it was not, for although she had written secretly to the postmaster at Mount Vernon to forward her letters, none had been received, and she knew there must be some reason for his ceasing to write.

At last she ventured on a little loving letter to him, but by freak of fate it went astray, and the lover's heart lost the joy it would have brought.

At length there came letters for Alva from abroad, and then she said to Floy:

"It was all true about my brother, mamma says. He has been very, very ill with brain fever, and came near to death."

They were sitting alone in the twilight, so Alva did not see the corpse-like pallor of the listener's face as Floy clinched her dimpled hands together in her lap, silently praying Heaven not to let her cry out in her anguish and betray her loving secret.

"But," continued Alva, "the crisis passed the day they reached London, and my brother is slightly better. The physicians say he may recover—unless he has a relapse."

Floy could not answer one word. It was all that she could do to keep her reeling senses from failing altogether.

George, her heart's love, her idol, ill unto death, and parted from her by the breadth of the terrible sea! Oh, it was cruel, cruel!

And she dared not cry out to this woman, his own sister:

"Pity me, sympathize with me, for I love him, he is my own, my own, and if he dies my heart will break!"

Not one word of grief must she utter unless the tidings came that he was dead.

Then she might open the floodgates of her love and despair, for betrayal would not matter when he was gone.

But she sat like a stone in the twilight of the room, so cold, so white, so still, and waited for Alva to say more.

Alva was in a bitter mood, that came to her sometimes when the memory of her past was revived.

She had been struggling to repress herself, but all in vain, for now, half forgetting Floy's presence, she cried out with passionate indignation:

"If he dies, that poor boy, my brother, his broken heart and early death will lie at his mother's door!"

32

FLOY LEANED FORWARD and clutched Alva's arm with icy fingers.

"Oh, for God's sake, tell me what you mean!" she faltered, imploringly.

"Why, what is it to you, child?" exclaimed Alva, startled out of herself by Floy's emotion.

"Oh, nothing, nothing, pardon me, Miss Beresford. But I was so sorry for you and for *him*, for—for you spoke of a broken heart," sobbed Floy, drawing back in dismay.

Miss Beresford was silent one moment, then she reached out and caressed Floy's golden head with one jeweled hand, while she answered:

"I am not offended, Floy. You startled me from a painful retrospect, that was all. I did not mean to answer you rudely, dear."

And loving the girl like a younger sister, perhaps craving her sympathy in this sad hour, she threw reserve to the winds and poured out her brother's story.

Nothing was kept back, his letter telling of his love, his mother's anger, her cruel reply, then the brief renunciation of the outraged son.

"Was he not brave?" cried Alva, with kindling eyes. "He threw away everything for Love's sake. Would that I, his sister, had been so true to self."

"You! you!" cried Floy, in tears and wonder.

"Hush! hush! I did not mean to refer to myself!" cried Alva, and sure as she was of the girl's sympathy, she repented of her momentary self-betrayal, and wrapped herself in a mantle of reserve.

A grief may ease itself with tears to start,
Or vehement outcries in passion's breath.

*But the calm stillness of a broken heart
Is sadder far than death.
Life may flow patiently in tearless wave,
Its palmless martyrdom concealed, secure;
Only the soul itself the grief may know,
And silently endure.
"The strength of all regret is lost in sighs,
In murmuring sorrow's fiercest flame expires;
But silence is the close where memories
Burn with undying fires.*

There was silence for a little while. Floy was fighting down the ache in her heart so that her voice would not betray her when she spoke.

Then she breathed, timidly:

"This illness of—your brother's—its cause?"

"His trouble, of course. He was in love with a beautiful girl, but he loved his parents well also, and he was his mother's pride and idol. She would have thought a princess unworthy of him."

"Oh, Heaven!" thought Floy, despairingly.

"This very journey my brother took to Europe," continued Alva, "was planned by mamma to break him from a fancy he seemed to have for the beautiful Miss Maury of Mount Vernon. We did not admire the girl, and mamma was wild at the thought of having her for a daughter. But Maybelle was angling for him so skillfully that mamma had papa to telegraph him to come home, to go across the sea at a minute's notice." She sighed, and added: "You can see from this one incident how resolute mamma can be when roused to action. And as for papa, he always takes sides with her in everything."

"Perhaps—perhaps they will persuade your brother to desert his love," breathed Floy, tremulously.

"Perhaps so, or perhaps he will cling to her in spite of all, and in either case he will be unhappy," returned Alva, not dreaming how cruelly her words stabbed Floy's loving heart. She continued, sadly enough: "You see, if George marries the girl, they will disinherit him, and he will have so little money, poor fellow—having been used to luxury all his life—that he will not know how to live. Poverty will crush him, and perhaps he will regret that he ever saw the girl. Ah, me! Will you ring for lights, please, dear Floy?"

33

GEORGE BERESFORD'S precautions that his parents should not know of his illness were useless.

It was not probable that the son of an American millionaire could fall ill in London without the knowledge of the ubiquitous reporters for the American newspapers.

So the first news the Beresfords had of their son's illness was brought through a special to a New York daily paper.

Something seemed to snap like a too hardly strained cord in the mother's heart when she read the paragraph and she fell in a heavy swoon to the floor.

The thought had struck through her mind that if her son died it would have been through her pride and harshness that it had happened.

She had been too imperious and too hasty. She should have tried gentler means with her spoiled but noble and loving boy.

She realized it all too late as she cried out to her anxious husband:

"You must take me to my son. He must forgive me before he dies!"

"We will start at the earliest possible hour," he replied, huskily.

Most fortunately a steamer was leaving New York that day, and they had no difficulty in securing a first-class passage.

"It will be lonely for you, dear, without us. Perhaps you had better go on to Newport next week, as we had planned," they said to Alva, who answered, cheerily:

"No—no, I will await your return here. I am not anxious to begin the gay season at the seashore."

So she remained in the large, splendid mansion with the servants, and the anxious parents set out on their journey.

Oh, those weary days upon the sea, how long they were, how heavily they dragged to those two hearts aching with remorse and grief!

"We were too harsh," sighed the father.

"It was all my fault," sobbed the mother. "If I had pleaded for my boy you would have yielded, for your pride was not so great as mine."

"And, after all, the girl might not have been so objectionable. She was a poor girl," he said, "but poverty is not a crime, dear."

"No—no, and we have wealth enough to spare as a royal dowry for our son's bride. But, oh, the doubt as to whether she is pure and worthy! —for George is a noble son—it is that which tortures so cruelly. Oh, why did he not tell us who she was, that we might have judged for ourselves."

"It may be that he feared our interference with the girl during his absence."

"And he was right, for had I known where to find her, I should have bribed her, if possible, to give up her claim on George—yes, to go away and hide herself until the affair blew over," confessed Mrs. Beresford, frankly.

And had anyone told the proud lady that she had employed a high-priced detective to seek the girl her son loved, and bring her home to the Fifth Avenue palace, she would have thought they had taken leave of their senses.

The weary journey was over at last, and they reached London.

Soon they were bending over their son's sick bed.

But alas! it was enough to break their hearts, that sight.

The lethargy of that terrible illness following on acute delirium held the patient in its grasp, and he did not recognize the fond, anxious faces that bent over him, his ears were deaf to their words of love.

This condition continued for days, and they feared that the patient would sink into death without knowing the remorse and penitence they had crossed the sea to pour into his ears.

34

OH, THOSE DAYS and nights of sorrow and suspense! The tortured parents would never forget them.

The memory of their harshness was a lash to conscience that never ceased to sting.

In the weary nightly vigils, when they hung over the sufferer's bedside, the mother prayed, unceasingly:

"Oh, God, give me back my boy, that I may atone!"

All her pride was brought low. If she could have known where to find the mysterious girl her son loved, she would have dragged her by force, if necessary, to her son's bedside, hoping that the sight of her beauty would lure him back to life.

Oh, the strength of a mother's love! What will it not endure and yield and suffer for the sake of the beloved one!

The proud woman learned, in that fiery trial, all the strength of her love for her son—knew that it was stronger than pride or ambition, mightier than death.

"Give him back that I may atone!" was her continual prayer, until it seemed as if God must have heard and pitied at last.

The day came when he opened his heavy eyes and knew his mother.

They lightened with a faint gleam of pleasure, and from that moment he began to convalesce.

Memory lay dormant in his mind for days, but it wakened at last, as she knew by the sudden change on his face.

It was twilight, and the windows were open, that warm summer evening, to admit the pleasant air. The western sky was still faintly roseate with hues of the fading sunset, and the sounds of the London streets were softening with the close of the weary day of toil.

George had gone out for a walk, and the mother and son were alone.

She sat at the head of his low couch, softly stroking back the dark hair from his high, white brow with her jeweled slender white hand.

It made her heart ache to see how thin and wasted he was, and to think that her cruelty had wrought the change.

His hollow dark eyes were turned toward the open window, watching the rosy-purple sky with a far-off look.

Suddenly she saw his whole face change as with a spasm, and his lips contract as with pain. She knew that memory had reasserted itself, by the anguish in his eyes.

Impulsively she stooped and pressed her lips to his brow, and it was not all her fancy that he shrunk from the caress.

"My son!" she cried, entreatingly, but there was no reply, and she continued: "Forgive me!"

She knelt down by his side and put her arms around him. The proud, beautiful woman had never humbled herself like this to any one before in all her life.

"George, listen to me," she murmured, tremulously, but he could not speak. She felt his whole form shaking with emotion.

She cried out, tenderly:

"Oh, my son, I see that you remember everything, and you shrink from me. You feel that I was hard and cruel, and I know now that I was wrong, that I had no right to write you that cruel letter. My heart almost broke when I heard of your illness, and I came to you at once—your father with me—to tell you that we repent our harshness and wish to atone."

No answer yet, and she felt the wasted form heaving beneath the touch with heavy, repressed sobs that it seemed unmanly to utter.

"George, do you understand me, my dear?" she murmured, tenderly. "We repent our harshness, we withdraw our objections to your marriage. Whoever the girl is—and we feel that she must be good and pure, or she would not be our son's choice—we will take her to our hearts for your sake."

She paused for his answer, but it was only a succession of heavy sobs, such as can only burst from the breast of a man who gives up the struggle against emotion and lets the storm sweep him away.

It was a tempest of grief before which the grieving mother was appalled.

She put her arms around him and wept with him in passionate sympathy.

George stole back to the room so quietly that neither heard him. He hovered over them in perplexity of grief.

At length he saw that the tempestuous sobs were stifled by a manly will, and George answered, faintly, to his mother's implorings:

"Alas! it is too late."

"No, no, my son! Do not grieve my heart with such cruel words!" she cried. "You will soon be strong enough to come home with us, and then you shall marry when you will. Shall I write to Alva to seek out your betrothed and bring her home to greet you when we return?"

A strangled sob shook the invalid's form.

"Oh, mother, how good you are to me—just like an angel! I forgive all that there is to forgive, and—there will never be any more discord between us, please Heaven. I shall never have any one to love henceforth but you three—for—for—*she* is dead!"

"Great Heaven!" cried his mother, in amazement.

"*She* is dead," he repeated, with the calmness of despair. "That was the secret of my sickness, dear mother. They wrote to me just after I sent you my last letter, that she was dead—my pure, beautiful little love! There, I cannot talk of it even to you, dear, and—but there is father with a letter."

35

GEORGE, WHEN HE saw himself discovered, advanced to the bedside.

He was a tall, portly gentleman, with kind brown eyes and a pleasant face that beamed with joy as he said:

"A letter from Alva at last!"

His wife sunk back in her chair and eagerly perused it. Then she handed it to her husband, and turned again to her son.

"I suppose Alva is at Newport?" he said, trying to bring his thoughts back from the painful theme that held them—the loss of his darling.

But it was hard to remember anything else now, when sorrow was at its floodtide, sweeping like a torrent over his heart.

"No, Alva is at home. She will not leave New York till we return," his mother returned.

"But she will be very lonely, I fear."

"No, she is very busy painting, and Alva loves art better than society, you know. Besides, she has a companion—a lovely young girl whom she has employed as a model."

Alva's letter had not been very long, and she had chronicled the finding of Floy in one careless paragraph:

"Floyd Landon was so fortunate as to find Cupid the very day you left the city, and brought her to me at once, so I hope to finish my picture before your return."

George, in his bitter despair over Floy's supposed death, took no interest in his sister's pretty model, and Mrs. Beresford, of course, had no idea that her son's sweetheart was domiciled beneath her roof, while her lover mourned her as dead.

The mere utterance of her name by George would have solved the mystery, and saved him hours and days and weeks of pain, hastening his recovery by the force of joy, for the influence of mental emotions on the bodily health is too well known to be disputed, and the effects of grief and sorrow in breaking down health and retarding recovery are especially significant.

So the long summer days waxed and waned until it was well into July before the invalid's tedious convalescence became confirmed enough for him to be removed from his room to a pleasant place by the sea. Here he remained for a week, gaining strength more rapidly, and at last asking to be taken home.

A fancy had seized him to revisit the scenes made sacred by their connection with his lost love, and to find her lonely little grave, unmarked perhaps by monument or flower, and to raise a costly stone above the spot.

But he did not confide these thoughts to his parents.

The subject had never been revived between them again.

George had a bitter, secret consciousness that he did not have their sympathy in his sorrow, and that at heart the death of his betrothed was a relief to them.

Mrs. Beresford had indeed hinted to her son that a certain fair English dame, a dainty Lady Maud whom he had met the previous year, was not indifferent to him, and would be a very welcome daughter-in-law.

But her son had answered, with the indifference of ill-health and an aching heart:

"I would not want her though she were 'the daughter of a hundred earls!'"

And his father had whispered to his wife:

"Leave the lad alone awhile. His grief is too fresh and new to bear consolation yet. Time will bring the only balm—forgetfulness."

So when George renewed the subject of going home, they did not say him nay.

They, too, were anxious to return, and by the middle of July had engaged their staterooms on a steamer of the fastest line.

Bidding farewell to all their little coterie of English friends at Brighton, they were soon en-route for home and Alva.

George was gaining strength but slowly, and his large, dark eyes looked out of a wan, pale face, whose expression was too sad for tears.

This homecoming was inexpressibly bitter to his tortured heart, and his pale, grave, handsome face made him an object of romantic interest to all the lady passengers.

But he did not reciprocate their interest, he cared nothing for black eyes or blue that looked at him with gay coquetry or tender sympathy.

He said to himself that since Floy was dead he could never love again.

He held himself moodily apart from every passenger but one.

This was a blonde nobleman of barely middle age, very handsome and grave-looking—Lord Alexander Miller, who had recently inherited by his father's death a grand estate in Devonshire.

He was going over for a tour of the States, he told the Beresfords, but his grave blue eyes had in them a look as if he should not enjoy anything very much, the look of a man with some secret sorrow tugging at his heartstrings.

Perhaps it was this secret kinship of sorrow that drew the two men together on shipboard, for each recognized a subtle affinity in the other, and so they became fast friends.

There was something, too, in the nobleman's fair, frank face, so debonair though so serious, that fascinated the younger man. Where had he seen such blue eyes before in the dim past?

It came to him at last with a shock of mingled pain and pleasure.

His new friend bore a subtle, haunting, charming likeness to his dead love Floy. And for this likeness George admired him all the more.

By the time they reached New York, George was loath to part with his fascinating friend.

He pressed him to become his guest. The reply startled him.

"I shall be most happy to visit you later on, but for the present I am going to Mount Vernon, New York, where I have—friends."

It was a startling answer to George, who had also planned an early trip to Mount Vernon.

Why he wished to go he hardly knew, except to revisit in silence and sorrow the places sacred to his brief, ill-fated love-dream.

"As for the Maury's, they need not know I am there. I shall not call, for I despise that scheming Maybelle," he decided, remembering how falsely she had told Floy she was engaged to marry him.

But he did not tell the nobleman that he also was soon to visit Mount Vernon. He parted from him with frank regret, expressing the hope that they might soon meet again.

Then they went on shore, and there was Alva radiant with joy to meet them.

She had come down in the carriage to meet them, and tears flashed into her bright eyes as she looked at her darling brother so pale, so changed, so sad.

Her mother had written to her simply that her son's love affair was ended forever, making no mention of the girl's death, and Alva had been very indignant, saying to Floy:

"Mamma has made him give up his love. I feared she would, but I hoped George would hold out against her arguments. I see how it is. He loves mamma so dearly—never son adored a mother so blindly—and she has made him think that the girl is unworthy of him."

Floy choked back a rising sob, and sat like a statue in her chair, fearing to breathe lest she betray her cruel secret.

She was as proud as she was beautiful, this willful little Floy.

In the long happy weeks since she had been here with Alva she had dreamed some happy dreams, but now they were all over.

At first she had been glad to be here with her lover's sister, and she had pictured to herself over and over his joy when he should come home and find her here an inmate of his home, a pet with his loved ones. Surely, then, it would be easy to win their liking for his chosen bride.

But when Alva's confidences showed Floy the overweening pride of the Beresfords, she began to be frightened even of charming Alva.

She said to herself in weary nightly vigils:

"She, too, is proud, although she pretends to take her brother's part. I can see that she has little sympathy with unequal marriages. If she but guessed that I am the girl her brother loves, she would send me away from the shelter of this roof."

And in her terror of the cold world outside, her fear of her foes, and her longing to stay here till her lover's return, poor Floy held fast her wretched little secret of love, scarcely daring to breathe when Alva named her brother's name in praise or blame.

But that last conjecture of Alva's as to her brother's resignation to his mother's will nearly broke the poor child's heart.

She could not doubt Alva's word. It must be true that among them all, in their pride of name and place, they had turned his heart against her, his absent little love.

"He is fickle and false, my lover whom I trusted in so fondly! How can I bear this pain and live?" she moaned to her stricken heart, in the silence of her terrible despair.

36

BUT WE MUST digress a short while from the main points of our story to note what became of our villain, Otho Maury, after Floyd Landon and our heroine left him unconscious on the floor, to recover at his leisure from his long swoon.

Never was a villain assured of success in a nefarious design more cleverly checkmated.

In a few minutes after their departure, Otho revived, and lifted his head in wonder at his position.

A darting pain in his wounded neck recalled him sharply to a sense of all that had happened.

He had gone to Suicide Place to search for Floy, and found her, but she was armed, and had attacked him desperately with a murderous looking dagger.

He had swooned with the pain of the wound she gave him, and knew no more.

How long ago had that been? How long had he been lying here? And where was Floy?

He called her name faintly in the silence, but only the echoes of the grim old house gave reply.

"She has fled the scene believing that I am dead, curse her!" he muttered, vindictively, dragging himself up out of the slippery pool of blood beneath him, and dropping heavily into an arm-chair. Then he discovered, to his surprise, that his neck had been carefully bandaged.

Not knowing, of course, of the presence of the detective who had come upon the scene the moment after he swooned, he was filled with wonder at the fact that Floy had apparently bandaged his neck.

"But she has escaped me again! The foul fiend must have helped her to drive that blow into my neck!" he muttered, angrily, adding: "But she would not have found me such an easy victim—

I could have grappled with her and taken away the weapon—only that I was unnerved and trembling from the sights I had seen before I entered this room."

He shuddered and glanced fearfully at the door, as though expecting some unearthly presence to appear.

"Alone in a haunted house!" he muttered, fearfully. "I that always laughed at spooks and phantoms! But I shall never deny them again. I have stumbled by accident on the secret of this old house, and I know that it has its restless ghost. What if I could turn my knowledge to account, and—Ugh! what was that?"

He broke off, shuddering, for a fiend's laugh seemed to echo in the stillness—the laugh of a fiend who has tempted some poor soul to its eternal ruin. It was more than the unstrung nerves of the man could bear.

With a muttered imprecation, he seized his hat from the floor, where it was lying, and groped his way out of the dismal house into the sweet night air.

But as he closed the door and turned from the accursed threshold, that fiendish, mocking laugh seemed to follow him with taunting echoes down the road.

Slowly and painfully he made his way home, thankful that the pall of midnight covered the earth, so that none saw him in the blood-soaked garments he wore.

Going to Maybelle's room, he told her what had happened, and asked her to examine the wound.

Shuddering at sight of the blood, his sister carefully unwrapped the bandages, and found that the wound—a very slight one, though it had bled freely—had already been carefully dressed.

"Your swoon must have been a long one, to enable her to do all this before she fled from the house," said Maybelle, as she carefully replaced the bandages.

Otho was bitterly chagrined at the failure of his scheme and Floy's second escape from his devilish machinations.

"And the worst of it is that I cannot follow up her track for some time now. I shall be obliged to keep my room several days with this mark of affection she has given me," he growled.

Maybelle wept in bitterness of spirit, but she had no reproaches to offer him now. He had done all that he could, and was not to blame for his failure.

It seemed to her as if her lovely rival must indeed bear a charmed life, so cleverly had she escaped each time from the machinations of her enemies.

Her chances of ever winning Beresford grew each day less and less, but so madly had she fixed her heart upon him that it seemed to her without that hope she must die.

It was less than a year since she had known him, but her jealousy had altered all her life.

Before she met him, Maybelle had been simply a handsome, selfish girl, ambitious to make a grand match—even to secure a title, if possible.

Mrs. Vere de Vere had abetted all her desires, but no grand suitor had fallen into the net they spread until Beresford's careless flirting had awakened hopes never to be realized, and alas! roused the sleeping devil in a nature well-endowed with capabilities for evil.

What a potent factor is Love in all the affairs of life.

Laugh at Love, flout him as we may, he still is our master, we his slaves.

Not till Love comes in all his strength and terror,
Can we read other's hearts; not till then know
A wide compassion for all human error,
Or sound the quivering depths of mortal woe.
'Not till we sail with him o'er stormy oceans
Have we seen tempests; hidden in his hand
He holds the keys to all the great emotions;
Till he unlocks them none can understand.

Maybelle's unhappy love and thwarted ambition had roused all the worst passions of her nature. She would have committed any evil deed that would have won her Beresford's heart.

37

IT WAS A week before Otho could mingle with the world again in his search for the brave girl who had so strangely eluded him.

And then her disappearance became as strange as it had seemed the first time.

Naturally it did not once occur to him that Floy had found a powerful protector in the person of Miss Beresford.

The splendid house on Fifth Avenue, where the heiress lived, was the last one he would have thought of searching for the missing girl.

Yet in that splendid casket Floy, like some beautiful precious jewel, was hidden from his sight.

The fair girl in her modesty had refrained from acquainting her kind employer with the story of her persecution by Otho Maury. She thought:

"If I told her all, she might think me boastful and vain."

And she was too anxious for that lady's good opinion to run such a risk by lack of discretion.

She had even secured the detective's promise of silence on the subject.

"Do not tell Miss Beresford about that villain. You can simply say you found me at Suicide Place," she had urged while they were on the train coming to New York.

Thinking it could do no harm to keep the little beauty's secret, he consented to what she asked, and in his subsequent interview with Miss Beresford—in which she generously remunerated him for his time and trouble in finding her *protégée*—he made no mention of Otho Maury's dastardly persecution of Floy.

Floy on her part was equally reticent.

The fall from the window of her lodging-house, as told by herself, seemed a very tame affair.

"I lost my balance while looking down and fell into the street," she said. "As for my sensations while plunging through the air, they were simply indescribable in their horror, for, of course, I thought I was rushing upon instant death. But the newsdealer's shed broke my fall, and I rolled down to the pavement actually unhurt, though the shock of terror was succeeded by a long swoon, during which I was removed to Bellevue. When I revived alone in the waiting-room and found myself unhurt, I ran away, and what more natural than that I should hide myself in the only refuge that belonged to me—my old home."

She might have told her story, with all its romantic embellishments, to Alva, and made herself a very heroine of romance in that young lady's eyes, but she shrunk from doing so. She dreaded ridicule, perhaps disbelief of her strange story.

"I am safe from my enemy's machinations now, so I will spare him until I can pour the whole story into George's ears," she decided.

But Miss Beresford noticed that whenever she took the little beauty for a drive in the park, as she often did, Floy was always muffled in a very thick veil, through whose meshes even the keen eyes of love or hate could scarcely have detected her identity.

Miss Beresford remarked on this one day, and Floy faltered out something about sunburn and freckles.

"Oh-h, I see! You are afraid of spoiling that rose-and-lily complexion, and I can scarcely blame you," laughed Miss Beresford, whose rich olive complexion could bear well the kisses of the wind and sun. Then, as she saw how sensitively Floy blushed at her words, she added: "Or, more likely, you are shy of the admiring glances you would meet if unveiled."

Floy had no answer ready, for she did not wish to tell the lady that she feared to be recognized by an enemy.

38

SO, WHILE FLOY'S enemy sought her all in vain, the day of her lover's return came at last.

It was two months now since their parting at the cottage door, in the May moonlight, under the drooping vines that shaded the porch—two months since that last kiss of love so true and warm and tender.

The burning heats of July held the world in their hot grasp, and the little spring flowers were faded and gone, as were the tender hopes of Floy's heart.

But all that last day she busied herself, flitting hither and thither, helping Alva to make the house beautiful for the returning dear ones.

"My brother loves flowers, especially roses, most dearly, so we will have roses everywhere," said Alva.

Floy's heartbeat fast, and she flushed, then paled again, as she remembered that strange dream of roses—hers and George's—that summer night of their first meeting—the dream that had seemed to draw their hearts closer together.

"But his love grew cold before the sweet roses faded," she sighed from the bottom of her sad young heart.

Then something seemed to whisper tauntingly:

"He is rich, and grand, and handsome, and can choose from the proudest women in the world. You should have known from the first that you could not hold his fickle fancy—a simple little maiden like you."

As she passed and repassed the grand plate-glass mirrors she would look into them anxiously, and with dissatisfaction.

She saw that she was wonderfully lovely, that her hair was bright as spun gold, her eyes as blue as violets, her mouth a budding rose, her complexion as gloriously tinted as a rose-lipped seashell, her dimples entrancing—but after all it seemed to her a babyish kind of beauty.

She thought that the dark queenly style of beauty of Alva and Maybelle was hundred times more attractive than her blonde type of beauty.

Poor little Floy was sadly changed since she had heard that her lover's heart had grown cold.

She had lost the sauciness from her smile, the sparkle from her eyes, and now and then a low, repressed sigh heaved her tortured breast.

Miss Beresford could not help seeing the change.

It puzzled and perplexed her, until she said at last:

"You are not happy here with me, Floy. Perhaps I go out too often in society and leave you here alone. I will stay at home more hereafter."

"Oh, no—no, I am happy enough!" protested the poor child, who felt relieved when she was alone and could throw off the mask of indifference and let her tears flow unrestrainedly over her broken love-dream.

She was so young, so friendless, and this love had become a part of her life. She could not see how she was going to live with this aching heart.

But she could not own her sorrow to George Beresford's sister, never—never! She would go away and die sooner than that.

With her own little trembling white hands she carried the great basket of roses to his luxurious suite of rooms. She arranged every bud and flower to look their best for his eyes, and the single bud in the tiny crystal vase on his toilet-table she kissed twice, thinking:

"It is so sweet and fragrant he may perhaps wear it on his coat, and think of me."

Alva came in, and looked about her with delight.

"Why, Cupid, you have made it a bower of roses. Are you sure you have left any for me?" she laughed, admiringly.

"The florist said he would bring you some more," answered Floy, blushing because she had taken so many for her darling's room.

"Then you must finish the arrangements, dear, for it is time to go and meet them now, and you refuse to accompany me."

"Oh, I could not—I could not!" Floy cried, affrighted, and Miss Beresford cried, gayly:

"What a bashful child you are, Cupid!"

She was turning away when Floy caught her sleeve, and gasped, imploringly:

"You must promise me one thing. I shall not see them tonight. You will let me keep my room till tomorrow, and not send for me to come down this evening? For—for—of course you will have many things to talk of, you four, and a stranger would be in the way."

Alva saw that she was painfully in earnest, but she thought it was only girlish bashfulness. She smiled indulgently, and said:

"Perhaps you are right. We shall have much to talk of, and it might not interest a gay little girl like you. Besides, they will be tired and will retire soon, so you may easily be excused till tomorrow."

She hurried down to the waiting carriage, and Floy, with one last tender glance about the room, went to her task of decorating Mrs. Beresford's suite of rooms, her heart heavy with pain as she thought of the proud, rich woman who had come between her son and his heart's true love.

When they came at last, Floy was at her window, peeping between the lace curtains for one furtive glance at the beloved face, and when she saw him step from the carriage at last, so pale, so wan, so ill, like a wraith of her debonair lover, it almost broke her fond, pitying heart.

39

ALVA WAS RIGHT about the travelers being weary. They retired early to their rooms that evening, George first of all.

"How sweet, how beautiful!" he cried, when the odor of the roses greeted him from every side.

He went up to the table, where a half-blown bud in a slender crystal vase charmed him with its crimson beauty.

"What a rich, warm, velvety scarlet rose—the flower of love!" he exclaimed, and pressed his lips on the curling petals.

In that instant a memory of Floy, his lost young love, came to him in bitter agony.

He turned his head quickly toward the door.

It had seemed to him that he heard a long, low, quivering sigh behind the shadowy *portières* of violet silk.

And as he looked he saw vaguely—or was it only fancy? —a tiny hand all white and dimpled, gleam an instant on the shining silk, then vanish.

"Alva!" he called, thinking she had followed him for a tender little chat.

But there was no reply.

He sprung to the *portières* and thrust them aside, but the long, brightly lighted corridor was empty.

He returned to his room slowly, thinking in a solemn awe:

"It was not my fancy. I distinctly saw a little hand—small, white and dimpled—vanishing away. It was *her* hand—my Floy's—beckoning me to the world of shadows."

All night, whether waking or sleeping, she was in his thoughts—his dead love.

The odor of the roses, their bloom and beauty, had recalled her to his mind as she had been the night that he had dreamed of her among the roses—blessed dream that had sent him to her side to save her from deadly peril!

She was with the angels now—lovely little Floy! —but she had hovered near him tonight. He knew by the little welcoming hand that had gleamed there a moment among the folds of violet silk.

Dear little hand! How he had loved its dimpled beauty! How soft and warm and thrilling it had been when he pressed it! Alas! it was only an icy shadow now!

"Dear Heaven, I wish that I might die and follow little Floy to her bright home!" he groaned, despairingly.

Small wonder that his sleep was restless and disturbed, and that in the morning he was wan and hollow-eyed as some pale ghost.

Alva was shocked, but she did not tell him so. She only showed her concern by the tenderest care.

"We must take you down to Newport before the end of the week. New York is stifling now," she said, with a significant look at her mother.

"Yes, I am very anxious to get away from here," rejoined Mrs. Beresford, promptly, as she rose from the table, adding: "I suppose your 'Cupid' is finished, dear?"

"Yes, and you must all come and pronounce on its merits," replied Alva, leading the way arm in arm with her brother.

George had to profess a polite interest he did not feel as they entered the studio and stood before the favorite picture.

"Where is she—your lovely model? I had forgotten her until this moment!" cried her mother.

"I will send for her," returned Alva, speaking to a maid who was in the room.

The girl went out, and then Alva turned to her brother, who was gazing with startled eyes at the beautiful canvas.

"That face! that face!" he exclaimed, pointing wildly.

"I painted it from life," she replied, adding, proudly: "Can you imagine anything in life so perfectly beautiful?"

40

ALVA LOOKED INTENTLY at her brother, and she saw that he was struggling with deep emotion.

It pleased her to see that her picture could affect him so deeply.

"Is it not beautiful—the face of Cupid? Can you imagine anything living so perfectly beautiful?" she repeated.

Slowly, without taking his eyes from the lovely face, George replied, dreamily:

"Yes, I can imagine it, for I knew the original in all her living beauty, the fairest among women. Oh! my sister, how exquisitely you have reproduced her upon canvas! This picture must be mine, mine only—all that is left me of poor dead Floy."

They drew close to him—father, mother, sister—and Alva caught his hand.

"What is that you mean? Have you ever known this girl Floy— my lovely model?" she exclaimed.

Half impatiently, as if amazed at her stupidity, he answered:

"Have I not told you that she was mine—my little sweetheart Floy, that the angels took away from me?"

"Floy Fane?" almost shrieked his mother, and he answered, wearily:

"Yes, did you not know?"

And so they stood face to face with the truth.

Bonny little Floy, the lovely Cupid of Alva's picture, was George's sweetheart, whom they had hated and reviled—without knowing!

The shock was so great for a moment that no one could speak, they simply looked at one another with joy, and wonder in their eyes.

They loved Floy in their hearts for her beauty and sweetness and pride. Oh, if they had only known it sooner, how much sorrow had been spared his suffering heart! Even their pride could not have rebelled against that lovely bride.

Mrs. Beresford found voice to exclaim:

"Why did you not tell me her name? Why did you say that she was dead?"

Something in her face and voice so startled him that, with his unstrung nerves, he could not stand upright. Sinking heavily into a chair before the picture, he looked up at her in wonder, answering bitterly:

"Why need I have told you her sacred name when I knew that you would only execrate it because my darling was a poor girl and not in the 'set' you adore? Besides, where was the use? She was dead, poor little Floy!"

They gazed at one another questioningly, wondering how they could break to him the truth that Floy was alive and well. In his nervous, enfeebled condition, how would the shock of joy affect him?

The father, with the usual masculine dread of scenes, kept himself in the background, leaving it all to the two women.

Mrs. Beresford's heart swelled with joy as she thought that now was the moment in which to atone for all her cruelty.

She had been bitterly despondent over her son's low spirits and failing health.

She had fancied sometimes, in her trouble, that the spirit of the beloved dead girl was drawing him by invisible threads to rejoin her in the spirit world.

Against that subtle power of love she had felt herself so impatient that she could have cried aloud for mercy, in her wild despair.

Then, what joy, what relief, to know that the girl was alive—a girl, too, so fair, so young, so innocent that she need not be ashamed to present her to the world as her son's wife.

Her face fairly beamed with joy as she bent over him asking, tenderly:

"My son, who told you that Floy Fane was dead?"

41

GEORGE LOOKED UP at his mother, and it angered him to see the look of joy on her face.

"She is so glad—so glad of my darling's death that she has not the grace to hide it, to feign a sympathy she cannot feel," he thought, miserably.

"Answer me, dear," she persisted, grasping his arm in her excitement.

He turned his heavy eyes on her face, and said, reproachfully:

"You need not look so glad that she is dead, mother. My grief is bitter enough without that. Well, it was Otho Maury, if you wish to know who wrote me she was dead. He sent me a paragraph from a daily paper. She died by accident—fell from a fourth-story window. Oh, God!" he ended, with a groan, putting his hand upon his eyes as if to shut out some terrible sight.

Mrs. Beresford drew back at her son's reproach, and signed to Alva that she could not go on. It must be her task to break the truth to her brother.

She knelt down before him. She put her arm about his shoulders, and her dark eyes, when she raised them to his face, were streaming with tears—tears through which the sunshine of joy broke gladly, as she exclaimed:

"Dearest, we have news for you—joyful news. Can you bear it?"

He started, his heavy eyes flashed with sudden hope.

"Speak!" he cried, hoarsely, and she answered:

"Florence Fane did indeed fall from the window—the paragraph told the truth—but Otho was mistaken about her death. She—she—lives!"

"Lives?" he cried.

And they never forgot the joy that transfigured his face. It was like sunshine suddenly breaking through a dark cloud.

But in a moment he added, sadly:

"She lives? How can that be? Perhaps you are going to tell me that she is a wretched cripple for life?" and the anguish of his voice was heart-rending.

She studied his face gravely, then asked:

"Would that make any change in your love for her, my brother?"

Trembling with emotion, his brain whirling with the shock of joy, he answered, fervently:

"Change? Yes, I should love her all the dearer, my suffering little love, because to my devotion would be added the divine elements of pity and sympathy. Where is she, Alva? Take me to my darling at once! Ah, now I can live again in her life! I will be her strength and shield. I will watch by her couch of pain, and soothe her in her sufferings!"

Overcome with emotion, he leaned his face on Alva's shoulder, and a stifled sob burst from his lips.

In that moment they all realized in its greatness the might of his love for little Floy.

Alva glanced around to see if Floy were coming in answer to her message.

What a moment it would be when she should take the fair young girl by the hand and lead her to George in all her enchanting beauty!

Several moments passed, yet the door did not open.

Alva guessed now all the cause of Floy's timidity, but she wondered at the girl's delay.

If she really loved George, why did she not hasten to his side?

Lifting his head from her shoulder, he asked again, eagerly:

"Where is my darling?"

"She is here in this house, George, alive, uninjured, more beautiful than ever. I have sent for her. She will be here in a moment."

"You have planned all this to surprise me! Oh, what a joyful moment!" he cried, with his eager eyes on the door.

"No, it is you who surprised us, dear. We knew her only as my model. How could we guess she was your little sweetheart whose name you did not tell? And as for her, she did not breathe her secret."

"Because I bid her not," he explained.

And while they waited with burning impatience for Floy to appear, they told him all they knew of the fair girl who had so interested his mother from the first moment of their meeting.

George listened with breathless interest to every word, his heart throbbing with joy, his blood bounding through his veins with new life.

"If you had only written me her name, dear, all this trouble would have been avoided, for Floy won my heart at our first meeting, and I should not have been able to steel my heart against the little beauty!" cried his mother.

"And you will welcome her as a daughter?" he asked.

"Proudly," she answered, smilingly.

"And you, father?"

Mr. Beresford laughed, and answered, blandly:

"My son, I have always been under petticoat government since I married this proud lady, your mother. Her indorsement of your choice secures my consent."

How bright the future looked at that moment to them all!

But the next instant Alva's maid entered the room with so grave a face that it instantly sobered the happy party.

"Where is Floy?" cried Alva, impatiently.

"Oh, Miss Alva, I wish I could answer that question, but—but I've been all over the house—everywhere—and she's not in it. And then I went back to her room and searched more closely, and I'm afraid she has gone away, for—I found this note for you, miss," answered Honora, in real distress, as she presented her mistress with a square blue envelope addressed in Floy's hand.

42

ALVA TOOK THE letter from Honora amid cries of dismay from them all.

She broke the seal, and as she opened the letter, a flashing diamond ring fell out into her hand from the closely written sheet.

"It is the ring I gave her when we became engaged," exclaimed George, taking it and kissing it in memory of that night, his heart thrilling with the memory of her beauty and sweetness as he kissed her good-bye beneath the drooping vines.

Alva read aloud, knowing how impatient they would be to hear the letter:

"'DEAR MISS BERESFORD—I have gone away because there is a secret I can no longer keep from you, and I know that when you learn it you will be glad I left you.

"'I am the poor girl whose engagement to your brother so bitterly outraged the Beresford pride.

"'When I first came to you I was very happy, because I fancied I might win your love, so that you would welcome George's choice.

"'But when you told me his story, although you seemed to take his part, it seemed to me that you sympathized with your parents and feared that your brother would be unhappy in the lot he had chosen. You said he would be so poor he would regret that he had sacrificed fortune for love's sake.

"'At first I did not believe it. I was resolved to cling to my lover, and put his constancy to the test.

"'When you told me that your brother's love affair was over, that you believed that your mother had persuaded him the girl was unworthy, I fancied you were glad.

"'So I knew there was no use staying on for his return. His heart had turned from me, and he would be sorry to find me here.

"'I, too, am proud, though not a Beresford. There may be other pride than that of wealth and place.

"'I, little Floy Fane, the daughter of a most unfortunate race, born to a heritage of sorrow, poor and alone in life, am yet too proud to thrust myself upon a family that despises me, yet whose equal I feel myself to be in all but money—that mere dross to a truly noble heart.

"'So I have left you forever. I am glad that I have been of some use to you. I pity you and love you, for it seems to me that pride has made shipwreck of your own life. Love has no part in it, and you are not happy.

"'Do not feel troubled over my fate. Thanks to your generosity, I have money enough to support me till I find work again.

"'This ring—your brother's gift to me in the hour when I promised to be his wife, not knowing his family's pride and his own fickle heart—please return to him with a last farewell from

"'FLOY.'"

The letter bore date of the evening before. She had waited—poor little loving heart—for one sight of him, her fickle, lost love, then she had stolen away, alone and lonely, to begin her battle with the world again.

It was a cruel disappointment to them all, but they bore it bravely, because it did not seem possible that Floy could hide herself from them long.

Indeed, she had not even threatened to hide herself, for how could she suppose they would search for her in her exile?

She had told herself most bitterly that they would rejoice at her flight.

"Oh, the proud little darling, how cruelly she misunderstood me!" cried Alva, tenderly. "But we will send for Floyd Landon. He will find her for us as he did before."

43

THEY SENT FOR the detective and confided the whole story to him, knowing that he was both clever and trustworthy.

Mr. Landon was pleased when he heard that beautiful Floy was George's chosen bride, and he was confident that he could find her again.

But he did not judge it expedient to keep his promise to Floy any longer—the promise to shield Otho Maury.

So he said to the anxious lover:

"You have a dangerous rival."

"You mean Otho Maury?"

"Yes."

"Floy hates the villain."

"Yes, and he knows it. That makes him all the more dangerous, because he is determined on revenge for her scorn," and the detective related the story of that night when he found Floy at Suicide Place.

"That man will bear watching," he said.

"Then watch him for me, and if he harms one hair of my darling's head, his life shall pay the forfeit!" cried the angry lover.

It hurt him bitterly that he was not strong enough yet to join Landon in the search for his darling, but still, he had every confidence in the detective's ability, so he prepared to wait with what patience he could for tidings.

Meanwhile, his heart was filled with a great, glad joy at the news that she was living.

She was living, his beautiful darling, and she loved him still! He knew it in his heart that she loved him still. Such love as theirs could not change or falter from its allegiance.

Their hearts had met in a love that could not change or die.

It was only a little misunderstanding that had come between them—a little misunderstanding brought about by pride—that could easily be explained away once they met again.

"And I shall scold her just a little for doubting my faith," he resolved, thinking that Floy's belief in him should have been absolute even through absence and estrangement.

"And yet I know, past all doubting, truly—
A knowledge greater than grief can dim—
I know as he loved, he will love me duly;
Yea, better—e'en better than I love him.
"And as I walk by the vast calm river,
The awful river so dread to see,
I say, 'Thy breath and thy depth forever
Are bridged by his thoughts that cross to me.'"

Meanwhile, the very thought that Floy was alive was like the very elixir of life to him.

It did him more good than all the doctors in the world, with their pills and potions, could have accomplished.

"I shall get well now. I feel stronger already!" he exclaimed, gladly.

Several days passed without news from the detective, but he would not permit himself to be cast down.

"She will soon be found, my little love, my blue-eyed darling! I will be patient, I will wait, for when I find her again, we shall be parted no more, save by death itself!" he exclaimed.

They had talked it all over, and agreed that when Floy was found, George should persuade her to marry him at once.

She was friendless, homeless, and the sooner she became one of the family, the better.

There would be a nine-days' wonder over the marriage, of course. But no matter, they were prepared to risk it, in their eagerness to make up to the young lover for all the pangs he had suffered.

Alva made him welcome in the studio, where he spent more than half his time.

The picture of Cupid, and the half-finished one of Maidenhood charmed him, and beguiled the long hours of waiting for Floy to be found.

He was surprised one day to receive a letter from Maybelle Maury.

She knew that he had come home at last, but she did not know that Floy had been hidden in his home all those weeks, so she hoped that the hapless girl had dropped out of all their lives forever. Perhaps she had committed suicide, after all?

The very madness of love and longing drove Maybelle into a most unwomanly act.

She fancied that by thrusting herself upon the young man's notice she might reawaken in his heart the tenderness she had fancied was dawning there just before his meeting with Floy.

She wrote a tender and pathetic letter, in which all her heart was revealed.

"You are home at last," she wrote. "Oh, how glad I am to know it! Need I tell you how cruelly I suffered when I heard that you were ill far, far across the sea? I longed for the wings of a bird to fly to you, and hover near you all unknown. Would I have been welcome if you had guessed I was there? Ah, George, once I believed I might be all in all to you, but a cloud came between us. It was the last day of the picnic, and I have never understood why you left us so strangely that night, with only a note of farewell. Why was it? Will you not explain now? Was it my fault? Did I offend you in any way? If I did, surely I have a right to ask in what way? For surely you knew how kindly I felt toward you. But I must not say too much. Surely you understand the feelings you awakened in my heart. Forgive me for writing, but I am so wretched! Otho says you were only flirting with me, but I cannot believe it. Your dark eyes looked too earnest. But I implore you to write. Let me know the cruel truth if you really meant nothing by your words and looks. The certainty of despair is better than the cruelty of suspense.

"MAYBELLE."

She thought she had written a very crafty letter, and that he could not have the hardihood to doom her to despair. He would believe that Floy was lost to him forever, and be willing to go back to the old fancy.

At any rate, she knew that George was too honorable to betray her secret to the world. Whether he accepted her love or not, he would never reveal to anyone that she had proffered it to him unsought.

He did not belong to the low type of manhood that goes about with coat-pockets bulging with silly love letters from silly women, reading them aloud to whoever will listen, and boasting of his conquests among the fair sex.

Such a contemptible poltroon makes a high-minded person exclaim with Shakespeare:

"Oh, for a whip,
To lash the rascal naked through the world!"

St George was the soul of white-handed honor. He burned Maybelle's letter to ashes, and no soul ever heard from him that she had stooped from her pedestal of womanly reticence to write such words.

And he wrote back, courteously:

"I am sorry that you have misunderstood me, but your brother was right. I never had any serious intentions toward you, and thought it understood on both sides that we were engaged in a very harmless flirtation. Need I remind you that I never sought you, and that my brief visit at your home was as your brother's friend, and at his repeated solicitation?

"I thank you for the regard you have expressed for me, but I hope you will withdraw it and bestow the treasure of your love on one more able to reciprocate the gift. It may be best for me to own that my heart is irrevocably given elsewhere, and that I shall soon lead a bride to the altar."

And so with cruel kindness George strove to pluck the thorn of love from Maybelle's heart.

For love is often a thorny flower,
It breaks, and we bleed and smart;
The blossom falls at the fairest,
And the thorn runs into the heart.

The thorn had pierced deep in Maybelle's heart, and it almost drove her mad, that letter.

She sought Otho with it, and confessed the failure of her scheme.

"He despises me. I can never—never win him. And I think I hate him now. I would like to wound his heart as he has wounded mine!" she groaned, in her misery.

"Let him go. There are others as well worth winning," he said, angrily.

"But how am I to win them?" she cried, bitterly. "Listen, Otho: do you know that papa will surely fail next week? The panic has ruined him, and we shall be beggars. Mamma told me all to-day, and she said she had hoped I would have caught a rich husband before now. I could not tell her how hard I have tried and failed. And how cruel it will be to be poor! I would rather die!"

Otho looked at her closely. He had a pale, nervous look, and his eyes gleamed with a sullen fire.

Leaning close to her, he whispered:

"I have a plan to get money, Maybelle. Would you be willing to help me?"

"What could I do?"

"You would have to run a terrible risk, be sure of that. But my nerves are strong as steel, and yours, too, are they not?"

"Yes—yes, I am no baby. Tell me your plan, Otho.

"There is no danger for us, I am sure," he repeated reassuringly to himself, then in low, whispered words he told her his story.

44

BUT WE MUST turn our attention from other interests for a while to follow the fortunes of our unhappy heroine, lovely Floy.

How sadly her fortunes had altered since we first saw her flashing through the streets of Mount Vernon on her bicycle, a vision of beauty, light of heart, and careless as a joyous little hummingbird!

Love and sorrow had come to her as it comes to many, hand in hand, saddening her heart and changing her life.

Her life in those weeks with Alva had been widened in its scope. The clever and intelligent Alva had taught her many things.

Bitterest of all, she had learned how wide was the gulf of pride that yawned between her, a simple poor girl, and the heir of the Beresfords.

Self-exiled in her pride and poverty, she stole away from her luxuriant home that summer night, her blue eyes blinded by heavy tears, her heart aching in its desolation, yet with no thought of turning back from the conflict that lay before her in the struggle for existence.

In that slender, lovely form was embodied indomitable pride and strong self-will.

Her heart swelled with bitterness against George Beresford, who, after pretending to love her with such entire devotion, could be so easily swayed from his allegiance by another's will.

"He was not worthy my love!" she cried bitterly to her heart, as she flitted along Fifth Avenue in the glare of the lights, but so plainly dressed and heavily veiled that none could notice the wonderful beauty that might have attracted unwelcome admiration.

As her flight from Alva's protection had been carefully planned ever since she had heard of George's projected return, Floy had made sure of a refuge that, though lowly, would be safe and secure.

In a humble quarter of the city, not very far away from the Beresford mansion, lived a poor woman who made her living by lace-mending and embroidery. The Beresford ladies frequently employed her, and Floy had seen her a number of times during her stay with Alva. She knew that the woman lived alone very quietly with an aged, bed-ridden mother, and she had made private arrangements to go and board with this humble soul for a week until she could make arrangements for her future.

To this humble home Floy made her way without accident of any kind, and was welcomed by Ruth Bascom, the spinster lace-mender. That night the restless little golden head was pillowed on straw instead of down, the luxury of yesterday exchanged for the poverty of today.

She sat upon the side of the hard cot looking about her with a bitter smile, wondering why fortune was so unequally divided in this world, and if the Beresfords deserved wealth and happiness any more than she and the Bascoms did poverty and pain.

A passionate wish came to her to meet the Beresfords on equal grounds—to be rich and grand, to wear jewels and laces, and dance at their grand balls.

"They would not pity and scorn me then—they would be glad for their son to marry me," she thought.

The wish grew into a longing as the sleepless hours wore on.

Visions came to her in the long, sultry night—so close and hot in the stifling little chamber that she could not rest—of how different life might have been if only the wealth that had become only a tradition in the family now had not been so strangely lost.

"I should be his equal now. No one would try to part us, and—we should be so happy!" she sobbed, and the bitter, bitter tears came in a burning shower.

She buried her hot face in the pillow, shuddering, for a wild temptation had come to her—one from which she shrunk in terror.

She murmured, faintly:

"It is a terrible risk, but what matter? Life is not so sweet that one should greatly prize it, even if goaded to throw it away!"

But she hid her face in her hands, and her slight frame shook as with a mortal chill.

A vision had swept over her of the day when she had found her beautiful mother cold and dead—dead by her own hand—

and how she, a weeping child, had been taken to the hearts of the good, kind old couple who had loved her so dearly.

"If I died, there would be none to weep for me—none but dear Mrs. Banks," she thought, piteously, and the terrible temptation to risk life for the sake of sordid gold overpowered the poor girl who had never realized till now the worldly value of the hard, yellow, shining metal.

A yearning to be rich and grand like the Beresfords, to meet them on equal grounds, to give them scorn for scorn, to flaunt before their eyes the devotion of other lovers, overpowered the unhappy girl, who knew that there was one chance in a hundred of realizing these radiant dreams—one chance which she vowed to strive for despite the grim records of sixty years of her ill-fated race.

It was August now, and ten years had passed since a victim had been immolated on the grim altar of the Moloch of Suicide Place. Would it claim another sacrifice, this insatiable monster? But a few months of the fatal year remained.

"Whom the gods wish to destroy they first make mad."

45

AH, HOW SLOWLY pass the days and weeks when parted from one we love!

> *Oh, absence is the night of love,*
> *Lovers are very children then,*
> *Fancy ten thousand feverish ills*
> *Till their loved one returns again!*

Beresford knew all the meaning of the poet's plaint as the slow days and nights dragged their weary lengths along without tidings of Floy.

For, though a week had passed away, Landon had no encouraging news to give.

The suspense began to tell on the weakened nerves of the impatient lover, and his improvement became less marked as hope and expectation became dulled in his heart.

But in vain they urged him to desert the hot city for the cool breezes of Newport.

"It would seem like deserting my darling. I cannot go until I find her," he answered, resolutely, and so the burning August days found them lingering still in the city, though the aristocratic avenue was deserted save for them. They would not leave him there to fret and grieve alone over his trouble.

He was bitterly impatient over his lingering weakness that prevented him from taking an active part in the search for Floy.

"Be patient, dear. Mr. Landon will surely find her soon!" Alva would exclaim each day, her own heart aching in sympathy with his pain.

She brought from Floy's room, for his eyes to feast on, the books the young girl had read and marked, and it was a melancholy joy to him to read every line her dear eyes had rested on or her pencil marked. It seemed to bring their sundered hearts closer together.

One day she chanced on a little blank book in which Floy had been wont to scribble her girlish fancies when alone, and she found that many of her sweet thoughts had been clothed in poetic diction.

Poetry is the natural language of love, and Floy, in her sorrow, had fallen so often into this tender speech, that Alva's tears fell like rain as she read the simple lines.

There was one little poem that bore date the very day of George's homecoming, so she could not doubt that it was written for her brother.

"Who would have dreamed that bright, arch little Floy had such depths of womanly tenderness in her nature?" she exclaimed, when telling George about the sweet little verses.

"You will let me see them!" he cried, eagerly, and Alva assented, saying:

"Yes, for I am sure they were composed by Floy herself, and intended for you, my dear. They are very simple and sad, and perhaps have but little literary merit, yet they breathe the love and constancy of a noble heart."

She gave him the little book to read, and he turned the pages as though they were something sacred, for here and there they were blistered with Floy's sad tears.

The letter that Floy had left for Alva had told but little of her love, and breathed only her indomitable pride. How different was the little book that in her hurry she had forgotten to take away!

Every tender word found an echo in George's devoted heart, and when he came to the page that bore date of his homecoming, he was not ashamed of the tears that rose when he read the sad and tender lines so full of her love and sorrow and tenderness.

YOU WILL KNOW.
When lighter loves shall fail you in your need,
When the prop you lean on proves a broken reed,
When wrong and falsehood cause your heart to bleed;
When all the world seems hollow, cold, and dark,
When for one tender voice you vainly hark,
When quenched in night seems Love's ethereal spark;
And when, heart-broken, you remember me,

The love forsaken in youth's wanton glee,
To roam the wide world fickle, fancy free;
And you return repentant and forlorn,
Shamed in your soul that ever you were born,
Scarred with the lash of heartless worldings' scorn;
And when you find, despite the cruel past,
The patient heart that held your image fast,
Forgiving all, then you will know at last;
How I have loved you, how my heart has kept
Its faith through unfaith, though of joy bereft
When naught but hope and memory were left;
How I have loved you when I dry your tears,
And calm your wild remorse and anxious fears,
And point your hopes to brighter future years.

George read the sad words over and over till they were imprinted on his memory. They had the greatest fascination for him in their hopeless love and sorrow.

He tried to write some verses in reply to them, but after many efforts he was chagrined to find that he did not possess the least poetic faculty. He could rhyme "love" with "dove" to be sure, but the lines were not even.

He threw aside the pencil, crying, tenderly:

"Oh, my little love, how cruelly you have misunderstood me! But only let me find you again, bonnie Floy, and I will show you that I, too, can love with changeless constancy."

But oh, how far away that blessed time seemed, for Floyd Landon failed to find any clue to the beautiful runaway, and at last he appeared at the house saying rather abruptly that he wished to give up the case.

46

BERESFORD COULD FIND no words in which to express his surprise and chagrin.

He could only stare, speechlessly, at the detective waiting for an explanation.

He saw that Landon looked pale and nervous.

"You are ill!" he exclaimed, at last, as if that explained all.

"No, I am not ill, but—I—have had—a great shock—so that I cannot bring myself to go on with the search for Miss Fane. You must employ someone else."

"But who can succeed where you have failed, Landon? You, the bravest, cleverest detective in New York!"

The detective smiled, as if gratified at this praise, then sighed:

"You would not call me brave if you knew all. You could hardly credit it, that a New York detective, in this prosaic nineteenth century, could feel a fear of—the supernatural!"

He paled and shuddered as at some ghastly recollection, then continued:

"I am coward, I confess it, Mr. Beresford. I that never flinched at the sight of danger in mortal shape, have struck my colors and fled from—ghosts!"

"Explain!" cried the young man, anxiously, then seeing the extreme pallor of his visitor, hastily rang for wine. "Drink. You will feel better," he said.

Landon gulped down half a glass, and the color returned to his pallid face, as he said:

"I have been searching Suicide Place again for Miss Fane."

"Yes?" eagerly.

"I have not found the missing girl, Mr. Beresford, but I have learned that the gossips of Mount Vernon told the truth when they declared that Suicide Place is haunted by evil spirits!"

Every word dropped separately with awful emphasis, and Landon's face, white and solemn, with deep, troubled eyes, attested his implicit faith in his own declaration.

Beresford was too shocked to reply. He waited mutely for more.

Landon drained his glass, and continued:

"When I had searched New York vainly for a week, I concluded that Miss Fane had perhaps ventured back to Suicide Place. I went down there three days ago. The very first night I made a startling discovery."

"What?"

"I found that Otho Maury and his eldest sister, the beautiful Maybelle, were in the habit of spending the wee small hours of each night secretly within the portals of Suicide Place."

"Great heavens! for what sinister purpose, Landon?"

"It occurred to me that they had somehow imprisoned Miss Fane in the house, and were keeping her there to force her consent to a marriage with Otho, who is madly in love with the little beauty."

"It is very probable. But you—you found out—"

"No."

As that strange word dropped from the detective's lips, Beresford glared at him as if he would spring at his throat.

"You—you dared to come away and leave her to their mercy, you coward!" he groaned.

Landon paled and shuddered, but he fronted the other's wrath fearlessly, answering quietly:

"I am not angry at your harsh epithets, for—my God! how can you understand?"

"Explain then before I leave this house to go to her assistance!" thundered Beresford, in deadly anger, overcome by the thought of Floy in the power of her relentless enemies.

What would they do to her, his hapless darling? Would they kill her, or, perhaps, more terrible still, force her into an abhorred marriage with Otho Maury?

His senses whirled with his misery, and he was on the verge of falling, when Landon caught him, pushing him back into his seat.

"Listen to me one moment," he cried, and continued: "I have done that any man could do, but I have failed to follow the wretches to their lair. In that grim old house there is some malign influence that drives the bravest man back to the threshold half mad with horror. What is it? It is haunted, that is why! No, I have seen nothing, but—the spirits of the damned haunt that house as surely as we two live and breathe. If you could hear them, Mr. Beresford, those sounds of woe that echo through the long corridors and empty rooms, that fiend's laugh that chills your blood like ice, and drives you back, shuddering from the threshold, out into the cool darkness of the summer night so sweet and peaceful, you would no longer cry out coward. You, too, would turn and fly."

"Not I, Landon, not I. All the hordes of hell assembled could not frighten me back from my darling in peril!"

"You think so. Let me tell you what I have seen. I have watched them go in before me, Otho and his sister, and as I retreated they would rush past me in terror great as mine. I have seen her three nights fall swooning on the wet grass. He would revive her, coax her, and hand in hand, encouraging each other, they would re-enter, perhaps overcoming their fears, and remain for hours, always leaving before daylight and skulking home unseen. Braver than I, you say? Yes, but they were two, I was only one. At last I could bear it no longer. I came away. I ask no recompense. I resign the terrible quest."

47

FLOYD LANDON'S NERVES were so shaken by his experiences at Suicide Place, that no entreaties could induce him to go on with the search for Floy.

His usual clear head and steady nerves had apparently deserted him. The truth was, that he was on the verge of a severe illness that seized on him that night and prostrated him for several weeks.

When he was gone, the impatient lover confided all to his family, and announced his immediate departure for Mount Vernon.

"I shall take a posse of men and explore the old house by daylight. Not a nook or cranny shall escape me, and if my darling is hidden there, she will be found. Indeed, I cannot understand why Mr. Landon did not do this," he concluded, with feverish impatience.

"I cannot let you go alone. I will accompany you!" exclaimed Alva, eagerly, and the offer was eagerly accepted.

They started for Mount Vernon within the hour, and on arriving went at once to a hotel.

What was Beresford's astonishment to meet there a person whom, in the agitation of his troubles, he had almost forgotten— his interesting *compagnon du voyage*—Lord Alexander Miller!

The nobleman's fair, handsome face had acquired a deeper cast of pensiveness than before. His splendid blue eyes were grave and sad, but they kindled with admiration when they rested on the brilliant beauty of Alva as George presented him to his sister.

When he saw George's start of surprise, he smiled and said:

"I see you had almost forgotten me, George."

"Not so, but I was not expecting to meet you here—although I remember now you told me when we parted that you were coming to Mount Vernon."

"Yes, I have been here ever since, and am just now leaving. In fact, my cab is waiting for me at the door."

"Shall we not meet you in New York on our return?"

"Perhaps so. I have not forgotten your invitation, but I have felt too depressed to leave here before. The truth is, I came here expecting to see some dear—friends. But I have had a great shock. I found them dead."

There was a note of pain in his voice, and Alva's heart throbbed with a strange sympathy, he seemed so grave, so sad.

He resumed, after a moment, wearily:

"I feel so unsettled, I scarcely know what to do. My first impulse was to return to England, but I have been lingering on here till now, so I suppose I shall do America before I go home. My present plan is to go to Newport at the pressing invitation of some Americans I met last spring in London."

"We, too, go to Newport as soon as my business here is concluded, so we may meet again soon," exclaimed George, with real pleasure.

"I am glad of that—so it is *au revoir*, and not good-bye," smiled the Englishman, lifting his hat in farewell ere he turned and descended the steps to the waiting carriage.

Alva's eyes followed him with frank pleasure—not only that he was the handsomest man she had ever seen, but because something about him recalled to her the loved and lost one of her girlhood's dreams.

"How like, how strangely like!" she thought, with silent pain.

And somehow her thoughts followed him on his way with a kindly interest just for the sake of the frank blue eyes that had looked at her gently like the eyes of her dead lover—dead, but not forgotten.

And as Alva's thoughts followed him with a strange interest, so did the handsome Englishman's fancy return to her during his brief journey to New York, dwelling with pleasure on her beauty.

"What a magnificent creature! The most beautiful American I ever saw! There was soul in those large dark eyes—soul and feeling as of one who has suffered! But what sorrow could come to the beautiful heiress, Miss Beresford?" he wondered, with deep sympathy, resolving that he would be very certain to accept her brother's invitation, for the sake of seeing her again.

She was still in his thoughts, and his blue eyes had a dreamy look as he left the train and sought a carriage to convey him to a hotel.

It was late afternoon, and the great city was a Babel of noise and confusion.

Shaking off the spell thrown over him by Alva's charms, he leaned from the window of the carriage, watching the unfamiliar scene with curious eyes.

The next moment he became the witness of an accident that thrilled him with alarm.

A beautiful young girl, who had attempted to cross the street, had been knocked down by a reckless bicyclist, who, with shameless indifference to what he had done, hurried on his way ere he could be arrested.

The girl, who was carrying a small traveling-bag, as though on her way to the station, lay helpless where she had fallen, the blood trickling down her face from a cut on her white temple.

In a moment the Englishman had stopped the carriage. He sprung out and caught up the unconscious girl from her perilous position in the middle of the street in the surge of hurrying vehicles, and carried her to the sidewalk.

A knot of people gathered around, gazing in pity and admiration at the lovely face in its frame of rippling golden hair.

A compassionate woman took some water and bathed the blood from the wounded temple, exclaiming, angrily:

"It is a shame that that rude fellow was not arrested for running down this sweet girl! She might have been killed!"

She bound a soft white handkerchief about the wound, and continued:

"Does anybody know her? She ought to be taken home or to the hospital. Oh! so you are coming to, miss?"

The girl had indeed opened two large blue, wondering eyes upon the anxious group that surrounded her.

"Are you hurt much?" inquired the kind though loquacious woman, helping Floy—for it was our little heroine—in her efforts to rise.

Floy was now on her feet, but ghastly pale and trembling.

She answered, faintly:

"No, no, only my head. But I feel very weak. I—I must sit down a minute."

"Drink this," said someone, proffering a glass of water.

She looked up into the face of a fair, handsome man, and felt a thrill of subtle pleasure at his gaze.

When she had drained the glass, he added, kindly:

"My carriage is here. Permit me to take you to your destination."

Floy knew that it was not safe to trust strangers usually, but the voice and face of this one were so noble they inspired instant confidence, so she answered, gratefully:

"I will thank you very much," and, with a grateful smile at the woman, she followed him to the carriage, saying: "I was on my way to the station, to go away, but I feel so shaken that I had better postpone my trip till tomorrow," and she named the address of Ruth Bascom, with whom she had been staying while she rallied her courage to return to Mount Vernon.

It was a long distance, and a sudden mutual attraction between them made the pair very confidential.

"I am so thankful your injuries are so slight. You might have been killed," he began, and the girl answered, sadly enough:

"It would not have mattered much. Life is so sad."

"Sad? For one so young, and—pardon me—so lovely?" exclaimed her new friend, in surprise.

Floy answered, out of the bitterness of her sad heart:

"I am only a poor orphan, sir, with no relatives and but few friends. To such a one life offers little happiness."

"That is true," assented the nobleman, with keen sympathy, and a great wave of tenderness swept over him for the lovely, hapless child of misfortune.

He looked at her simple dress, and guessed that she was poor as well as orphaned.

He, too, was almost alone in life, but he was rich, so he had many friends. We can always count our friends when we are rich.

She seemed little more than a child to this man of forty years, and he felt as if he would like to draw the golden head against his shoulder and tell her she should be his child, his dear adopted little daughter, if she would, and that poverty and sorrow, those grim twins, should never come near her anymore.

But he feared to startle her by an abrupt avowal of his benevolent desire, lest he should arouse distrust in her girlish mind, she looked so timid and innocent as she sat there by his side, so he decided not to speak to her abruptly of his wish.

48

HE SAID, WITH a long-drawn sigh:

"Life is sad to many, my dear little girl, and perhaps I have had as sad an experience as any."

She looked at him with questioning eyes, and, although he was usually very quiet and reserved, after the English nature, the lovely face drew him so strangely to her that he continued:

"Suppose we compare notes. I will tell you what a great sorrow I have had in my life, and then you may tell me your story."

Floy did not reply, and he saw her rosy under lip quiver as if she repressed a sob with difficulty.

She was thinking with pride and pain:

"I can never tell this kind and noble gentleman the story of my blighted love-dream. I do not believe that he could understand a nature so ignoble, so fickle as that of the handsome lover I trusted so fondly, and who failed me so cruelly in the end. His name shall never pass my lips either in praise or blame, although I never can forget him."

Her new friend continued in a clear, low voice, just audible above the rumble of their carriage-wheels on the stony street:

"But I have not told you who I am yet, so perhaps I had better introduce myself. My name is Miller. I am an Englishman, and but a few months ago inherited a title and large estate from my father, who was a peer of the realm."

"You are great and rich!" exclaimed Floy, and he caught a note of disappointment in her voice, and wondered at it.

He continued his story by saying:

"Wealth and position do not always bring happiness. They stood in the way of mine."

"And of mine," thought Floy, in silent sympathy, while he went on:

"Eighteen years ago—ah, me! how long it seems! —I was the heir apparent to my father, a powerful noble, and a member of parliament. I was his only son, and all his hopes centered in me. My mother was dead, and I used to spend much of my time with a favorite aunt in London, who had two charming children. I met there a beautiful American girl recently orphaned, who was employed as a governess. We loved at first sight."

"It is a great pity for the rich and poor to fall in love with each other. It cannot end happy!" cried Floy, out of the bitterness of her own experience.

"How cynically you speak! Has the world already made you so wise?" exclaimed Lord Miller, in surprise, but Floy blushed without replying, unwilling to betray herself further.

And again he took up the thread of his story:

"I see that you understand what a *mésalliance* it would be considered for the heir to a title to marry a poor governess, though she was pure as an angel and beautiful as a princess. I knew it all too well, but love would not listen to reason. I won her promise to be mine, and then, hopeless of gaining my father's consent to be married, persuaded my darling to elope with me. Her consent was hardly won, but she became my bride at a little English church, and we went to live in a pretty cottage home pending my forgiveness by my father. Alas! it was never to be won. My father cursed me, and drove me from his presence, swearing that I should never have a penny from him, and that I should live on the beggarly two hundred a year that I inherited as a legacy from my mother. My aunt was also obdurate, and would have nothing to do with us. In fact, we got the cold shoulder from all our former friends."

"The rich are as cruel as death!" murmured Floy.

"Not all of them, dear child, as I shall convince you by and by," returned Lord Miller, wondering what cruel experience had made her so harsh and bitter, and resolving that she should be his adopted child if she would consent.

She looked up at him with admiring blue eyes, and added:

"I am glad that you were brave enough to marry your love, in spite of the opposition of your rich relations. Not many a young man would be so brave and true."

He said to himself, shrewdly:

"This lovely child has had a romance in her life already. The pain of an aching heart throbs through her bitter little speeches. Her pride has been wounded by some vulgar rich person, no doubt."

And he looked tenderly at the little beauty, while he said:

"There are plenty of young men who would marry the girl they love in spite of the whole world. I am glad I was one of them, and I had two years of almost perfect happiness with my darling—two years in which a lovely little daughter came to us—a girl who would be about as old as you, my child, if she had lived. Alas! she is dead—she and her mother!"

His voice trembled, his face grew pale, she read keen despair in his dark-blue eyes.

"I must hasten with my story," he cried, mournfully. "I have told you I was happy with her only two years. Well, at the end of that time my father sent for me to come down to one of his estates in the country—a dreary place in Cornwall that we seldom visited, and that was half a ruin. We thought—my wife and I—that he meant to forgive us at last, and I went joyfully, for I did not know he had a heart of stone.

"I met him at that grim old pile of ruins, and he tried to bribe me to divorce my darling wife and desert my child. When I refused indignantly, he—can you imagine anything so horrible? —made his minions thrust me into a dungeon of the old castle, and swore to me I should die there unless I consented to his plan.

"I steadily refused, and I remained his prisoner almost fifteen years, while he gave it out to the world that I had wearied of my American wife and gone to travel in far countries.

"Is it not a wonder that my heart did not break in those cruel years? At last Heaven took pity on my tears and prayers, and stretched my inhuman parent on a bed of death. Then he had me brought to his bedside, and implored my pardon for what he had done, after confessing that my poor wife, believing his diabolical tale that I had deserted her, had eked out a toilsome existence for herself and babe in London for a few years, then returned to her native land, and he knew not what had been her fate thereafter.

"How could I forgive him his cruel work? I fell in a swoon by his bedside, and before I revived he died, and went to meet the judgment of the wicked. Then I set about finding my darlings. I wrote to her old home in Mount Vernon, New York, and received no reply. I searched London over for months, and with no success, so I determined to come to America. I went to my wife's ancestral home, Nellest Farm, and found it was deserted. I made inquiries, and learned that my wife, Mrs. Fane, as she called herself, had died the terrible death of the suicide ten years before—that my daughter Florence was taken care of by some kindly neighbor who only lately met death by a terrible accident!"

"No—no, I am your daughter Florence, dearest father!" cried Floy, in joyous excitement.

49

LEAVING FLOY TO explain matters to her newfound father, we must return to Mount Vernon and follow our hero in his search for his missing love.

At his hotel, which was located within a square of the Maury mansion, he found that the all-absorbing subject of conversation was of the disasters that had befallen the Maury family within the last twenty-four hours.

The great importing house of Maury & Co. had failed yesterday, and the head of the house had fallen dead of a stroke of apoplexy.

And following on this calamity to the devoted wife and family was the mysterious disappearance of Otho and Maybelle.

Last evening they had retired early to their rooms, seemingly prostrated with grief over the death of their kind, indulgent parent.

This morning they were missing, and no clue to them could be found.

When George Beresford heard this news his heart sunk within him in prophetic dread.

Knowing what he did of Otho and Maybelle's nocturnal wanderings at Suicide Place, he could come to but one conclusion.

Floy was their prisoner, as Landon had suspected, and fearing detection, they had spirited her away to another place.

"We have come too late!" he cried, bursting into Alva's presence in a quiver of emotion, and falling wearily into a chair.

"No—no, you must not tell me so," she exclaimed, with keen regret, and then he poured out the whole story.

Alva saw the situation in all its terror. She did not know what to say to her brother, but she saw that she must offer him some comfort to save him from utter despair.

He had grown frightfully pale, and the despair in his beautiful eyes made her heart ache.

It seemed to her as if his very life was bound up in his sweetheart Floy—as if the failure to find her would surely break his heart.

She could not permit him to give up hope, although she herself had almost lost heart.

"You must not lose heart like this. That old house must be searched!" she cried, with such cheerful eagerness that he was inspired with fresh courage.

"Then I will go at once!" he cried, starting up.

"The sooner the better," agreed Alva, and within an hour they were on their way, Alva choosing to accompany him, because she wished to be on the spot to solace his sorrow if he failed to find Floy.

She was determined to do all she could for him, openly blaming herself for the flight of the girl.

"It was my idle chatter to her that made her lose faith in him and run away, so I must do what I can to atone," she said.

At the very last they decided to go alone.

George remembered the gruesome character of Suicide Place, and how he had heard that no one could be persuaded to go there for love or money.

Besides, he shrunk from creating a useless sensation, for he had little hope now of finding his darling there.

"You know all the terrible things that Landon told me. Are you willing to risk the horrors of the place?" he asked Alva, anxiously.

Alva was a magnificent woman, in high health and with strong nerves. She laughed at her brother's question.

"I am not at all afraid that the ghosts will rout *me*!" she replied, gayly.

So they ordered a carriage to take them out, and the driver was almost petrified with astonishment when they told him to drive past Suicide Place.

It was nearing sunset when they reached the grim old building in its splendid grove of trees, and again the driver gasped with amazement when told to stop there.

"We are going to walk through that splendid grove," explained Alva, carelessly.

"But, begging your pardon, miss, surely you don't know what an awful name the place bears. I wouldn't set foot inside that gate for a thousand dollars, poor as I am!" cried the man, in consternation.

"Oh, yes, I *do* know all about the place, but I don't believe those spook tales, and my brother and I are determined to explore those grounds so that we can boast of our bravery hereafter. So you may wait for us here," laughed Alva, and she was vastly amused when she saw the disgusted man drive off to the opposite side of the road so as to be as far as possible from the place.

But as she went in through the gates, out of the glory of the August sunlight that flooded the west, into the heavy shallows of the dark grove, the smile faded from Alva's ruby lips, and a subtle premonition of evil began to weigh on her spirits.

As for George, he was remembering the first time he came here—that May night that seemed so long ago now, when he had followed Floy, warned of her peril by that strange dream, and saved her from the insults of Otho Maury.

How freshly it all came back—the sweet May night cool with soft spring rain, the breeze laden with odors of wet lilacs tossing their purple plumes against the windows.

How sweet she had been! how grateful, bonnie little Floy! He remembered, as if it were last night, their ride home, and how they had parted at the door betrothed lovers! He could still feel that sweet, dewy kiss on his lips in all its divine bliss, and he stifled a bitter groan as he remembered all that had come and gone since then, parting them so cruelly from each other.

He felt Alva shudder as she clung to his arm, and looking down at her face, saw that it was pale and grave, with somber eyes.

"Alva, you are ill, or frightened!" he cried, anxiously.

"No, no, go on!" she answered, urging him on, and trying to shake off her strange depression.

The spell fell over George, too, and icy fingers seemed to clutch at his heart. He muttered, in a strange voice:

"I—I am not a coward, Alva. I do not wish to turn back, but I have a feeling that we are going to confront—something terrible."

"Yes, yes, but—go on!" she whispered back, with white lips.

They moved slowly, arm in arm, around the winding walk toward the side of the house, as George had gone that first night, toward the side door.

Everything was so still they could hear the beating of their own hearts.

"The door stands ajar. Perhaps I had better go in alone. You are nervous, Alva," he whispered.

"Not at all, but the place has a depressing influence—doubtless from the stories told of it," she murmured, clinging to him, and, indeed, putting her foot first upon the threshold.

They went mutely along the gloomy hall, expecting to hear the silence broken by those awful demoniac shrieks of which Landon had told. But all was still—awfully still.

Close to them a door swung wide open. They stopped, and looked with curious eyes at *what* lay beyond the threshold—two bodies, white and cold in death, lying side by side in a pool of clotted blood that showed dark in the sunset light streaming through the open window.

50

IT WAS NO wonder that the fiends' laugh echoed no longer through the dark, grim halls of Suicide Place, since its awful Moloch had claimed the sacrifice of the sixth decade.

Beresford and his sister stood as if turned to stone upon the threshold, gazing in upon that awful sight, on which the sun's last rays flickered dismally, as if in pity.

No wonder Otho and Maybelle had not returned last night! No wonder their disappearance remained so deep a mystery! They lay here dead in that awful house where scarcely a human foot dared penetrate.

Otho's stiffened hand lay along the carpet, still grasping the weapon with which he had sent a bullet through his heart.

His handsome features, white as marble by contrast with his jetty hair and mustache, showed ghastly now, with the fallen lower jaw and the half-open dark eyes, that held frozen in their unseeing upward gaze an expression of hate, as if they had looked last on some abhorred sight.

It was a tragedy to shake the strongest nerves, and they turned with relief toward Maybelle, who looked more natural, her eyes and lips closed, only her stillness and corpse-like pallor betraying that death was there. Above her heart was a clot of dried blood that had flowed from a dagger-thrust given by her own hand, for just beneath her touch lay the shining steel.

Alva and George contemplated the awful sight in horror too deep for words. With their arms about each other, they gazed and gazed, shuddering and trembling with pity, for their generous hearts forgot the wrongdoing of the pair in sympathy for the strange fate that had overtaken them.

At last rousing himself to the exigencies of the moment, Beresford sighed heavily and said:

"We must go and tell the driver of this awful discovery, and send him back to Mount Vernon with the news."

They went to the driver, who was so astounded he could hardly credit the story.

Curiosity conquered his dread of Suicide Place for once, and he followed them into the gloomy portals to gaze with awe on the sickening sight of the two suicides, then willingly agreed to drive back into town to spread the news and summon the coroner.

Alva insisted on remaining with her brother.

"We have not found Floy yet, you know," she said.

"Shall we resume our search?" he asked.

"It would be better than remaining in this room," she shuddered, and was turning away, when her pitying gaze, that had rested on Maybelle's ghastly face, suddenly returned to it in amazement.

"Look—look!" she cried, wildly. "Her eyelids moved! See, her breast heaves! She is not dead! She revives!"

George turned back at his sister's words and saw that they were true.

Maybelle was reviving.

Her dark eyes opened wide and rested imploringly on their faces.

"Do not leave me!" she faltered.

They hurried to her side, and Alva lifted the heavy head on her arm while Beresford poured a few drops of wine between her lips from a flask he had brought with other restoratives in a tiny case.

Maybelle moaned faintly:

"Poor Otho, he is quite dead, is he not? His courage did not fail—like mine—at the last."

Beresford drew a shawl over the dead face reverently, hiding it from her sight, and she added:

"When the cold steel pierced my flesh it pained me so I could not drive it home to my heart. It fell from my hand and I fainted. But—but—I shall die all the same, shall I not?" anxiously.

51

"*OH, WE HOPE* not!" they answered, soothingly, and raised her gently, placing her on a soft couch by the window, where the summer breeze could caress her pale brow.

"Oh, how I have prayed and prayed for someone to come," she continued. "Ever since midnight I have lain here fainting and reviving, fainting and reviving, too weak to rise, and longing for water to cool my parched throat. Oh, thank you, thank you, how sweet and cool it is! Oh, what a wretched day! When I heard your steps and voices coming, I fainted from pure joy!"

She did not seem surprised at their coming. Perhaps she guessed in some way at the reason.

Beresford stooped over her with anguish in his eyes.

"I must ask you one question," he cried, "and as you hope for Heaven, if you die, I implore you, answer it truly. Is Florence Fane in this house?"

"She is not. That is true," answered Maybelle, growing paler at this reminder of her successful rival.

"Where is she, then? Do you know?"

"I swear I do not know," she replied, faintly, and he read truth in her beautiful eyes.

She was strangely beautiful in her pallor and pain, and Alva thought for a moment how strange it was that her brother had not loved charming Maybelle before he met Floy.

But in the next moment she sighed to herself:

"There is no accounting for Love's vagaries. I am glad my brother loved little Floy instead of imperious Maybelle."

Beresford looked at the poor girl with pitying eyes. The knowledge of her hopeless love for himself softened his heart, and he said, gently:

"Why did you attempt this terrible deed? What malign influence drove you to self-murder?"

She shuddered and closed her eyes. He thought she was going to faint again, and reproached himself for tormenting her by such questions.

But Maybelle opened her eyes again, and said, solemnly:

"I will tell you the grim secret of Suicide Place, for perhaps I am dying, and the story should be known, and the old building torn down to set at rest an unquiet spirit. Floy knows it all, I am sure, but I do not think she would ever tell."

"You may exhaust yourself," he objected, though his curiosity was on the *qui vive*.

"No, I shall not talk more than is necessary." She swallowed some more wine held to her lips by his hand, and began: "Perhaps you have heard that the owners of this property—Floy's ancestors—were very rich long ago?"

"Yes, I have heard of old Jasper Nellest who was so miserly, and yet died poor, and left his descendants nothing but this property that seemed afterward to be banned by a curse," he replied.

"Yes, that is the gist of the story," answered Maybelle, sighing. "That old man died rich, but he had turned all he owned into yellow, shining, golden coin. But he did not mean to cheat his heirs of their inheritance, only he died suddenly before he could tell them where the treasure was hidden. Well, his punishment is to haunt his old home, vainly trying to reveal the secret he carried to the grave."

"Can this be true?" cried Alva in wonder.

"It is true," answered Maybelle. "I have seen him again and again, and it is horrible!"

She paused and glanced half fearfully at the door, muttering:

"But, no, no—he will be shocked at the evil he has wrought, he will not venture back for long, long years. It has always been so, they say."

They listened eagerly, devouring every word, wondering if her strange story could be true.

"You doubt me!" cried Maybelle, reading their faces. "Well, I am too weak to waste words trying to convince you. I can only tell what I know in the briefest fashion."

She rested a little while, then resumed her story:

"This old man—this miser—has surely hidden his gold somewhere in this house, but he has not the power of speech, only of strange, demoniacal laughter. It is this way: Some night in wandering through the long corridor—always the long corridor—you come upon an old man chuckling, gibbering to himself. You stop, you stare in terror, and he spreads abroad his lean hands. You see grouped about him, as in a golden haze, open chests of golden coin—think of it, *great chests of gold!* —and the sight fires you with a mad longing to possess the treasure whose existence you thus discover. You gaze spell-bound, but the hideous old miser begins to laugh with hideous mirth, gloating over his wealth, till you fly in deadly terror from the scene. But alas! only to return, goaded by an awful desire to search the old place over for the missing gold. You search in vain, and the old miser seems to gloat over your failures with his demon laughter, and then—then—the rage, the fear, the baffled desire for the treasure—seem to combine to drive one mad, so that this"—she shuddered as she pointed at Otho's still form— "comes naturally as the awful *finale*. He—Otho—found it all out while seeking Floy, and persuaded me to come with him to seek for the chests of gold. Alas, alas!" and with a long, shuddering sigh she closed her eyes again.

Alva stroked the dark tresses back from the damp brow, and they looked at each other, she and George, with wondering eyes that questioned:

"Can this story be true?"

The young man looked from the chamber of horror out at the quiet sunset skies, and it seemed to him incredible that such things could be.

But in the face of all that had gone before, and of this present tragedy, he was not prepared to deny anything. He could only say to Alva:

"It is a strange story."

Everything began to grow dark in the room before Maybelle spoke again.

She looked wistfully at Beresford, sighing:

"I do not wish to die now, though all the best things of life have slipped away from me. But—but I seem to be sinking away."

"Have you any last words—any wish?" he began.

"Yes, one wish." She seemed to forget Alva's presence, or not to care. "Will you—kiss me—just once? —I have loved you so!"

Her voice was pathetic in its hopeless yearning, and Alva motioned him to obey. She knew that noble little Floy would not grudge this one caress to her dying rival.

So Beresford gave the one kiss that was a joyful memory in all Maybelle's future years.

For she did not die as she foreboded.

The room was filled presently with a curious crowd who heard in wonder the strange story, and then carried the dead and the living home again through the darkening twilight.

Otho and his father were buried side by side, and kind friends cared for the helpless Maury family. Mrs. Vere de Vere, always Maybelle's stanch friend, adopted the girl as a daughter, so she never missed the wealth she prized so much.

In time Maybelle made the grand match Mrs. Vere de Vere had schemed for so long, but it was long years first, and when she married the rich politician, it was for ambition, not love. All her proud husband's caresses were not worth as much to her as the memory of one pitying kiss.

THE BERESFORDS RETURNED to New York the next day sick at heart and dispirited, for the mystery of Floy's fate was more inexplicable than ever.

In twenty-four hours after their return Lord Miller's card was received.

Mrs. Beresford was out, and George was ill again from the fever of a baffled hope.

So Alva went down alone to meet the handsome Englishman, and their mutual attraction toward each other was strengthened by this interview.

His earnest sympathy with her brother tempted her to confide the story of Floy to his sympathetic ears.

He listened in wonder to it all, and then she ended with a sigh:

"He is ill again, my poor brother, and no mortal physician can heal the wound from which he suffers—the pain of hopeless love."

He looked at the bright, beautiful face, wondering how she should know so much of what she spoke, then he said, abruptly:

"I wonder if your brother would see me a little while if I could give him good news?"

"Good news?" she faltered.

"Yes, of this girl—this Floy Fane. I know where she is today."

Alva almost fainted with joy. He never forgot her looks of gratitude and her expressions of joy.

"Come with me!" she cried, and led him to her brother's rooms.

"I have brought you a physician with news to make you well!" she cried, radiantly, to the pale, languid invalid.

And then Lord Miller told them of his *rencontre* with Floy the night of his return to New York, and his discovery that she was his own child.

We must pass over their delight and amazement when the romantic story was all told, and he ended by saying:

"I left Floy at the hotel, very busy looking over a few thousand dollars' worth of finery she purchased yesterday, but if you both will return with me, I think she will be glad to see you."

"Are you well enough dear?" inquired Alva, looking at her brother doubtfully.

He leaned upon her, his face flushed, his eyes alight with joy.

"I am a new man. I do not feel as if I ever had been ill," he repeated, joyfully.

So leaving an explanation for their parents, should they return in their absence, Alva and her brother accompanied Lord Miller to the Fifth Avenue Hotel in search of Floy.

"And to think how near she was to me while I was breaking my heart over her loss!" thought the happy lover.

He wondered if Floy would be glad to see him again, and his heart throbbed a happy response. He had the greatest confidence in his darling's truth.

"Lady Florence is in her own parlor," said the servant whom Lord Miller asked for his daughter.

Lady Florence! How strange that sounded to Alva and George! Yet it was her rightful title now.

Little Floy was never to know again the ills of poverty and loneliness. All that she had sighed for in other days was hers now—love, wealth, position. Lucky little mortal!

She had been amusing herself all day trying on her new dresses and jewels, but after all they did not fill her tender little heart. There was an ache there all the time because of her grief for her fickle lover.

"I wish that he could see me now. This gown is so becoming," she thought, artlessly, rejoicing in the possession of the cool white robe so soft and billowy in its fine laces and streaming ribbons.

At that moment three people were at the door, and Lord Miller opened it without knocking.

"Oh, let us wait outside!" cried Alva, with a romantic impulse, drawing back as George crossed the threshold.

Neither do we want to make a third at the reunion of the long-parted lovers, reader, so we will wait outside with the other couple, for we can guess at all that passed. Haven't we all been there ourselves?

Ah! happy love! Is it not a foretaste of Paradise?

Lord Miller found that he had recovered his lovely child only to lose her again.

George was the most persistent lover in the world.

He pleaded continually for an early marriage.

"Floy is nothing but a child, barely seventeen. Wait till her eighteenth birthday," answered the fond father.

The lover was most unhappy over the year's probation.

"I cannot bear to lose sight of my darling again. I give you warning I shall follow you to England when you take her away— ay, to the world's end!" he protested.

Lord Miller answered, laughingly:

"I shall extend you a cordial invitation to be our guest at our English home for as long as you please," and with that the lover had to be content, for even his own parents, though they loved Floy so dearly, took part against him.

"It is right that her father should have her for a time," they said, and Floy, who adored her noble parent, was well satisfied to have it so. She knew quite well, the saucy little darling, that George would seldom be absent from her side in that year of waiting.

They would not sail for their ancestral home until October, anyway, for they had much to do in America.

For one thing, Lord Miller had to seek out his wife's neglected grave, and place a fitting monument above the gentle heart that his father's wickedness had driven wild with despair. The thought of all she had suffered would haunt Lord Miller with keen despair as long as he lived.

Then, too, a great force of men was put to work on Suicide Place, to tear it down stone by stone to the ground, that its haunting spirit should claim no more maddened victims of the craze for gold. Even the grove was hewn down, that the very site should be forgotten, and Lady Florence presented the farm to Mount Vernon to be turned into a pleasure park.

The chests of gold that had been seen in ghastly visions of the night by so many poor victims were found to be a reality.

They were walled up in stone beneath the brick flooring of the cellar, and contained riches to the amount of half a million.

It seemed like a ghastly legacy to Floy, and she tried to atone for the sin of old Jasper Nellest, by devoting more than half of it to works of charity.

She had seen so much of the world's poverty and sorrow while she was poor herself, that she knew how to pity and sympathize, and, better still, to lend a helping hand.

She did not neglect to search out the good Mrs. Banks, who was now adrift on the world since poverty had fallen on the Maury family, and oh! what joy it was to the kind soul to see Floy again, whom she had mourned as dead.

She rejoiced unselfishly in the girl's good fortune, and wept when she clasped her in her arms, exclaiming:

"You shall come and live with me now, and be rich and grand."

"Oh, dearie, I could never go away from Mount Vernon and my poor John's grave!" she cried in her simple, faithful fidelity.

Lady Florence wept with her as she answered:

"But I cannot stay here with you now, and I do so want to make you happy. I have plenty of money, you know, and I want to give you as much as you want."

"God bless you, my sweet child, for your offer. It will make my heart glad just to raise a pretty stone over my husband's grave, and to go back to live in the little cottage again."

Lady Florence gratified her simple wishes, and settled on her a sum of money that kept her in luxury a lifetime, with a stout servant to wait on her, and an elderly cousin for a companion.

"And next year, you know, auntie, I am to have a grand wedding at our English home, Earlscourt, and you shall promise me now that you will cross the sea with the Beresfords to see me married," continued Lady Florence, blushingly.

Mrs. Banks was very proud of the invitation, and many good people in Mount Vernon envied her because she was so loved by the earl's fair daughter. They forgot that she had earned it all by her goodness to the lonely orphan child when her friends were few, and when they had sneered at her girlish pranks and given her the soubriquet of Fly-away Floy.

Lord Miller would be very lonely when his daughter should leave him for her husband's home, and one day, when he was grieving over it, Floy, said, roguishly:

"Get Alva to stay with you when I come away. She would make a magnificent countess."

"The very thing that was in my mind," he answered, quickly, and before he left America he told Alva of his wish.

"If you can be satisfied with a second love, I will make you a devoted husband," he said.

And Alva replied with a like confidence:

"My first love, too, is dead, but you have won my heart. I believe that we can be very happy together," she admitted, frankly.

And because Lady Florence would need her so much in the year before her marriage, she consented to an early wedding, and sailed with them in October to her new home far across the sea.

The End.

The End

About the Author

MRS. ALEX. McVEIGH MILLER was the pen name of Mittie Frances Clarke Point (1850-1937). A self-made author who was ahead of her time, she transformed personal tragedy—the loss of her first husband and infant daughter—into a remarkable 50-year writing career. She wrote 80 novels capturing the experiences of American women during an era of social change, and established her financial independence at a time when few women supported themselves.

Despite adopting her second husband's name professionally, she left the marriage in 1908, refusing to accept his infidelity despite the social stigma of divorce. Her historic home "The Cedars" in West Virginia stands as testament to her commercial success in a male-dominated industry, while her journey from trauma to literary stardom to reinvention as a single working mother mirrors the experience of countless women balancing ambition with family responsibilities.

THE MYSTERY OF SUICIDE PLACE

BY MRS ALEX McVEIGH MILLER

BOOKS BY ITNA

Urban Gothic: The Complete Stories
Bruce Benderson

Fair to Look Upon
Mary Belle Freeley

Settlers Landing
Travis Jeppesen

Aaron's Rod
D.H. Lawrence

The Beads
David McConnell

@UGMan
Mark Sarvas

At Night Only
Christopher Stoddard

www.ingramcontent.com/pod-product-compliance
Lightning Source LLC
Chambersburg PA
CBHW010542100726
47903CB00011B/3101